Death to Blonds:

Stolen Judgment

A Clint Folsom Mystery

BarbarianSpy

www.BarbarianSpy.com

This book is copyright © habu 2013
Published by BarbarianSpy in 2013
Cover design © S Bush 2013
Cover images: All manipulated, naked man ©Les3photo8:
Dreamstime.com, man with gun ©chagall: Depositphotos.com
ISBN Print: 978-1-922187-28-4
All rights reserved

BarbarianSpy
Jindalee St
Toronto, NSW 2283
Australia

Death to Blonds:

Stolen Judgment

A Clint Folsom Mystery

habu

Author's Note:

The chronological fit for *Death to Blonds: Stolen Judgment* in the previously published Clint Folsom mystery series is after *Death in Eden*, the concluding book of the *Clint Folsom Compendium, Volume One* collection.

The Clint Folsom Mystery Series:
(Available in paperback and e-book.)

Clint Folsom Mysteries Compendium: Volume 1

Death to Blonds: Stolen Judgment

Clint Folsom Mysteries Compendium: Volume 2

CONTENTS

Chapter One: A Night to Forget

It had been a rough day. A witness in a high-profile gangster's trial had gone missing the previous night, and Detective Clint Folsom, along with other guys from Homicide had been called in to help the beat cops try to find him and get him to the courthouse today. The condition they'd found him in in a New Jersey landfill meant there would be no court appearance for him today—and maybe no court case, as he had been the star witness for the prosecution. So another night wasted away, and they were behinder than they were ahead.

Clint should have gone home this evening and slept it off, as he'd been given leave to do. But Clint was keyed up and bummed out, and so he'd done what he usually did in this situation. He went cruising the gay bars of lower Manhattan to both remember and to forget. Today it was The Dugout on Christopher Street, near the docks. It just felt like a docks day to Clint. When he was in the mood for rich, older men, he went to the bars in Chelsea. When he wanted it rough from a muscle man, he went down by the docks at the tip of Manhattan. This evening he wanted to feel something. He hadn't felt much of anything the previous twenty-four hours, knowing the search would be fruitless and once more the gangsters would win. He wanted to be touched—deep. And nothing touched him anymore short of rough sex.

It was a slow night in The Dugout, an on-the-margin club, where big guys mingled with the leather and bear crowd on weekday nights after the after-work Wall Street types had cleared out after hooking up, or not—a place where you didn't normally camp out. You either hooked up fairly quickly or you looked over the crowd and decided to try it out farther up into the Village. If ships were in, there might be something from guys in want coming off the ships or beefy stevedores ready to party after a hard day on the docks, though, so if you were looking for what Clint was looking for tonight, it was worth a shot. On these nights, the men from the ships and dock nights, the testosterone could get so thick in the air that men got fucked right there in the barroom itself on the tabletops. Clint was so keyed up that this was what he had in mind.

He had done it before, and all of the men gathered around, watching, licking their lips, and pulling on their meat while he was getting on a table top, Clint knowing that each of them wanted to be doing that to him—and then some of them following the first—gave Clint an added high. This pushed all of Clint's fetish buttons.

The club was in its waning days and there was a hard core of patrons who acted like they owned the place and smoked up a storm and were forever playing heavy-metal band music on the juke box at near-deafening volume. That usually sent Clint on his way as soon as he cased the crowd and saw the docks had been quiet that day. But today, although there obviously had only been a few ships at the piers, the regular crowd was taking the night off.

So Clint was taking his time, leaning against a stool with his back against the bar, nursing a beer, and checking out the room. Several in the room were interested in him. He was far enough away from the precinct and his usual haunts for them not to mark him as a cop, and, although now slightly past thirty, he was still to be considered "a real catch." And, since he was obviously surveying the room, he was understood to be attainable—by someone.

The most likely one he could see through the smoke covering the tables in the dimly lit room was probably a stevedore, judging by the muscles bulging below his armless T-shirt and what appeared to be an oft-broken nose. He was an ugly son-of-a-bitch, but if he was hung like he was built, he was pretty much the punishment that Clint was looking for this evening. Clint was an unabashed stereotype; he liked them thick and long. Clint's thrill was in making the big ones disappear inside him and to dig deeper.

The problem with this guy was that he hadn't seen Clint yet—or, if he had, he wasn't interested. There were a couple of young, foreign guys—probably eastern Europeans off a freighter—that the stevedore was all over. There was every indication that he was propositioning them both, and there was a good possibility that he wanted to take them together. He had the look of being capable of doing so, which was why Clint was interested in him. This was a "punish me" evening for Clint. If it had been two hulking stevedores on one slim, young sailor, Clint would have been even more interested himself. He was partial to attention from more than one.

Beyond this guy, the best possibility that Clint could see was a hunky guy standing at attention by a door leading to the back of the premises. He was suited out in black and was wearing sunglasses despite how dim the lighting already was in the bar. But he wore the suit well—a bulky chest tapering down to a slim waist and what looked like beefy thighs below. Clint couldn't tell whether he was playing cigar store Indian or waiting for his turn to go to the back. The detective had been here before, so he knew there were rooms at the back. He usually preferred going off premises to play out his fantasies, though—except for keyed-up evenings like this, where he was more in the mood to do it on a tabletop with others watching.

After surveying the room again, Clint's eyes went back to the man standing at attention by the door. With the guy wearing sunglasses, Clint couldn't tell whether the guy was checking him out too—but the detective would remain open to that possibility.

He would give it several minutes to simmer—or maybe develop, with more patrons arriving. He turned to the bar and worked on getting the attention of the barkeep. There was only one guy working behind the bar, and the orders were running him ragged even though the club wasn't filled. Clint worked hard at not being irritated he had to track the guy down, but once he'd caught the guy's attention, the bartender pulled away from what he was doing and came right to Clint.

"Another one like that one?" he asked. He was giving Clint the glad eye, obviously liking what he saw. And Clint wasn't going to complain, because the bartender had obviously stopped serving a couple of other guys to get to him. He couldn't resist saying something, though.

"Yeah, please, another one. You look swamped and the rush hasn't started yet. Somebody didn't show to work the bar tonight, or is management trying to save bucks?"

"Greg's around here someplace and will be back in a few," the bartender answered. "And another guy will be in before the place fills up. And, I gotta say you're a real honey. When more help comes on, maybe, if you're interested, I could pull away and—"

"Yeah, maybe, if I'm still here," Clint answered. He knew it wouldn't happen, though. The guy was the willowy, flouncy type. He'd obviously misread Clint. He probably wanted the same thing Clint did—and wanted it from Clint. That happened to Clint a lot. He just came across as a top. But that wasn't at all what he wanted.

Clint nursed the second beer. If nothing was happening by the time he finished this, he'd try another bar. But he really didn't want to have to work hard at this. He wanted something, and he wanted it now. It had been a rough day. In fact, it had been a rough week and month—he'd been working double time ever since he'd come back to the city from the detail with his old friend and lover, Peter Blair, down in that rich county in northern Virginia. Peter had it real cushy down there. And he'd pushed Clint hard to transfer down there where he was county sheriff—and to return to Peter's bed.

Each time Clint had a day like he'd had today, he found himself reconsidering Peter's offer more and more seriously. He'd given Peter a flat no, saying the offer of the bed and servicing weren't bad—Peter could cock rough and was built big—but Peter was under the thumb of the county politicos who demanded to be more equal than anyone else, and the action in Virginia just wasn't as exciting as it was in New York City. Of course, it was the excitement of the city's crime that was giving Clint a headache now.

He sensed movement out of the side of his vision and Clint turned his head in time to see a bottle-blond guy in his late twenties, cute and twinky, closing the door to the back and

12

walking around to the back of the bar. The statue guy standing next to the door had given him a good looking over and then had opened the door and gone into the back himself.

The blond was walking sort of bowlegged and had a glazy-eyed look about him for several minutes after getting behind the bar. He was working in slow motion to begin with, and those he was serving had to hail him more than once to get his attention. But he snapped out of it soon enough and started chatting up the guys at the bar, including Clint. And before Clint knew it, he had a third beer in front of him, so he decided to stay on until that was done.

The club was filling up now, and the prospects were increasing. Most of the men arriving were built and more of them were in leather. They all also were zeroing in on Clint after having assessed the room. By the time Clint was finishing off his third beer, a big bruiser of a Russian sailor type was at Clint's side, a hand on the small of Clint's back, and offering to stand him another beer. Another big, rough-featured but heavily muscled guy—quite apparently a friend of the Russian and maybe from one of the Baltic countries himself—was crowding Clint from the back.

Clint accepted the beer, thinking that these two might be just the ticket to scratch the itch he had. The Russian man's leather vest was open, revealing a well-muscled, hairy chest. That was OK with Clint too. The other hulk wore a tight T and faded jeans.

"You just lookin' for a drink?" the Russian asked, his voice growly and his mouth close to Clint's ear.

"I wouldn't have come in here if I wasn't looking for more," Clint answered.

The Russian took Clint's hand in his and moved it to his crotch. "This enough more for you? Or maybe I move too fast."

The man behind Clint had a hand squeezing one of Clint's butt cheeks. "Maybe we could do a two for one," he muttered. His accent was heavy, but Clint didn't have any difficulty understanding what he said.

"I wasn't planning on spending long to get what I want," Clint answered. "And I'm not disappointed in the possibilities."

"You take us both?" This from the guy behind Clint.

13

"I don't see why not. Here or do you have someplace you want to go?"

The Russian was about to respond to that, still holding Clint's hand to his crotch, when all three of them heard a door slam shut and turned their heads toward the back wall of the room. The man who had just walked through that door was tall and broad-shouldered. He was maybe in his late forties, but he was a massively built, body-builder-muscled man. A swarthy complexion and black curly hair—Sicilian was Clint's first thought—and he had a mean look in his face of getting what he wanted or else.

He let his eye roam around the room. Clint heard a little moan behind him, and sensed the blond bartender, Greg, shrinking away and down the length of the bar as far as he could go. Even the Russian and his friend who were putting the moves on Clint seemed to shrink away. The Russian dropped the hand holding Clint's hand to his crotch, and Clint moved his away.

The Sicilian man's eyes came to rest on Clint and his eyes slitted. A smile that didn't really seem to be a smile crossed the man's face. He was the veritable essence of power and evil.

Clint wanted him. He sensed that this man could give him what the two others together couldn't. He turned his body to face the man. The Russian, standing behind Clint now, put his hands on Clint's waist, and Clint leaned back into his body and gave the Sicilian a challenging look.

The dangerous-looking man took a couple of steps toward the bar, and Clint saw that the man who had been standing beside the door moved forward with him, a few steps behind the Sicilian. Both men looked over Clint's shoulder, and Clint could feel the hands of the Russian trembling. And then the hands were gone and the Russian too no longer was standing behind Clint. The other guy already had faded away.

The Sicilian walked up to the bar. "You look like someone. I know, you look like that big-time movie star what got killed falling off the Pacific Highway. You know, the guy in that beefy lumberjack movie." He snapped his fingers and the bodyguard behind him showed for the first time that he could speak.

"You mean Sloan? Scott Sloan?"

14

"Yeah, that's right. Scott Sloan," the Sicilian said, not taking his eyes off Clint. "And his last movie, *High Timber*. I saw the special cut of that." He almost winked at Clint at that revelation. The special cut of *High Timber* had been a graphic gay male version that now was a very, very expensive collector's item. "You ever hear you look like—?"

"Yeah, sometimes," Clint answered. He was rather tired of being told he looked like Scott Sloan, although it undoubtedly was a big reason men—and women—gravitated to him. There was a good reason he looked like the dead actor. Scott Sloan had been his father. Clint had come East to try to overcome that connection.

"Well, it hangs good on you. What's this piss you drinkin'? You got Black Label back there?" He raised his voice for this last statement to get the bartenders' attention. It wasn't Greg who showed up to answer that they had it, but the other bartender, who appeared immediately.

"What you do for a real man's drink?" he turned and asked Clint, his eyes piercing, his smile cruel.

"Whatever a real man wants," Clint answered.

"You take a real man's cock?"

Clint liked the directness of this man. "If it's big enough."

"You expect money?"

"Not if it's big enough."

The Sicilian smiled a toothy almost smile. "I like a piece of tail don't beat around the bush. We drink. Then you come with me." It wasn't a request.

Clint hadn't expected to be doing it in the back of a car, but it was a limousine and there was plenty of room—room enough for three when it came to the limo being parked in an underground parking lot and the bodyguard, who also was the chauffeur, being invited to join them in the back.

While the car was on the move, the Sicilian sat in the middle of the backseat and Clint rode his cock, facing him, while the Sicilian slapped him around a bit and choked him until he was turning blue. Exhausted and fighting for breath, Clint laid over on his side docilely along the backseat and hooked one heel on the top of the seat and leveraged off the ceiling of the automobile with the ball of his other foot as the Sicilian knelt between his legs

15

and rammed his staff up into Clint's channel again and again and again. His beefy hands went back to Clint's throat. Clint was so far out of it that he wasn't sure whether he was being taken in succession or together after the chauffeur was invited into the back.

Whenever he was about to drift off into unconsciousness, a vial of poppers would be waved under his nose and his eyes would pop open, a kaleidoscope of colors would revolve in his head, and he could feel the intensity of a cock working inside him again.

Toward dawn, the limo was on the road again, and when it stopped, he was pushed out onto the ground in the middle of a cemetery, legs still splayed open as they would be for some time before he could close them, and his clothes were thrown out on top of him. He rolled over as the limo pulled away and tried to sit up, but his head was spinning, his ass was on fire, and he just laid back down with a groan.

He was completely spent and totally satiated. It was exactly the punishing fucking that he had wanted.

This was Clint Folsom. Clint was what was known as a satyriasist—the male equivalent of a nymphomaniac. He was normal in most ways. He just needed to be fucked constantly to be satisfied—and in his case he was most satisfied when the fuck was rough. And such were his looks and animal magnetism that there was no end to men willing to fulfill his need.

This was how he punished himself for what he saw as a wasted life of disappointment, guilt, and regret. And this was how he forgot the cases that threatened to get at him. He hadn't thought about that broken young man they'd found in the New Jersey landfill the entire time the Sicilian and his chauffeur had been working him over.

Chapter Two: Similar Cases

Clint woke up—in his own bed—with the feeling of pressure in his head and across his chest. And then he realized he was awake because there was pressure down further too. His cock was being fisted and slowly worked. The pressure on his chest went away when he realized it was a chocolate-brown, brawny arm that was weighing him down. He pushed it off him with a mutter of "Oh fuck." The pressure in his head, he knew, wasn't going to start going away until he got to the medicine cabinet in his bathroom. The fisting of his cock he tolerated until he got his bearings better. He was rather enjoying that particular pressure. He turned his head. The beefy black guy in bed beside him had his eyes open and turned toward him. They had a questioning look in them. Clint didn't have any difficulty deciding what the guy wanted.

Clint didn't have the foggiest notion who this guy was. He could guess, though, what he had been doing in his bed, although fuck knew how he'd gotten there.

"Has anyone ever told you you look like—?"

"Oh, fuck fuck," Clint growled, not letting that sentence finish. He rolled away from the black guy and stumbled out of bed and to his bathroom. Sun was streaming through the gauzy curtains of his bedroom window and he could hear the street noise coming up from below the window. He'd lived better than this when he'd been with Brad and he could live better than this now if he wanted to—he was a regular million-dollar-baby. But going back to the way he'd been living before he'd won, and then lost, Brad was part of his punishment of himself for being alive when so many others, including Brad, were dead. So, what he had here was a main living room with kitchen L on the third floor above a neighborhood grocery closet and a bedroom small enough that it only took him three steps to reach his bathroom.

Once in the bathroom and having turned the lock on the door, he took a quick piss, flipped the top off a Listerine bottle, poured a slug into a glass, and swished it around in his mouth to try to get rid of the sour taste. The he leaned over the sink and stared at himself in the mirror. How the black guy out there could come up with him looking like any kind of movie star in this condition was beyond Clint. He did sort of like the swarthy look of the day's growth of beard, though, and thought maybe he'd keep that for a while. It would be classier if it was darker, of course, but he was cursed with being a natural California blond.

He reached for the bottle of Tylenol—what *had* he been doing that had him hung over like this?—and then reached over and turned on the shower to let the water heat up while he brushed his teeth in another effort to get rid of whatever that taste was in his mouth. It was a slightly musky taste, and that told him maybe he didn't want to dwell on what he'd been swilling around in there.

The door rattled and there was a knock on the door.

"You takin' a shower in there?"

"That or someone turned on Niagara Falls," Clint called through the door.

"You let me in and I'll shower with you. Show you more of what I can do inside you."

"I'll bet. I'll just be a minute. Meantime maybe you can find the front door."

"Ah, come on man. You were hot for it earlier. God, you were a good fuck. And, come on, let me in. I gotta take a piss."

"I'll be just a minute." Clint groaned. He wondered how many times they'd done it without him remembering any of it. The guy was a chunk; he didn't mind doing it with him. He just would have liked to have been there for it.

And he wasn't much more than a minute. As he came out of the door, holding a towel around his waist, the black guy, standing a good foot taller than Clint and a whole lot beefier, grabbed for the towel and whipped it off the smaller man. He

18

pulled Clint close with one arm around his waist and reached for Clint's cock and held both Clint's and his together in his fist.

"Shit, you have a body to die for," the black guy muttered. "Come on into the shower."

"I've just showered and you said you needed to piss," Clint answered, but he gave no resistance when he was pulled into the shower, the water was turned on, and he was pushed up against the back wall, facing the black hulk, with the guy pressed against him.

"I'm gonna be good to you again," the black guy growled as he palmed and spread Clint's buttocks; raised Clint's feet off the wet floor tiles, sliding Clint's back up the soapy tiles of the back wall; and settled Clint's channel on his cock. The cock was as beefy as the rest of him, and yet he slid right up into Clint as if he'd already reamed the space he needed. And, of course he had.

Good to me again, Clint thought as he sucked in his breath, lost now to the possessing cock as he always was when one slid inside him, especially when it was this thick. Wonder how many times he's already been good to me? And I don't even know who the fuck he is and what he's doing here.

He did, though, know what the black guy was doing here right at the moment. And he was doing it very well. Clint hooked his ankles around the small of the black guy's back, took the guy's head in his hands, and pressed their foreheads together, his not throbbing as much now as when he got out of the bed, thanks both to the Tylenol and the attention his body had transferred to his channel. Resigned to what came next, he established and maintained eye contact with his master. That's want Clint wanted when he got into this position—to be mastered.

"Oh, shit, yes. Fuck, fuck. Deep in. Oh, fuck, yessss."

The eye contact told Clint the guy was really, really enjoying being inside him. This was about as good as it got. The pumping stopped and the guy was trembling slightly. So was Clint. Then a long slide out. And in. And out. Clint began to pant.

"Now, dammit," he hissed through clenched teeth.

"Got chu now. You're all mine now," the black dude growled, slammed deep, and jerked twice as he filled up the head of his condom.

Clint started to lower his legs, but the black dude growled, "No, don't. Jus' gimme a minute or two. I do doubles."

"Oh, God," Clint whispered.

Afterward Clint left the guy finishing his own shower and went into the bedroom. He picked his towel up from the floor, dried himself off, and then pulled on fresh briefs from a bureau drawer and a pair of jeans. As he pulled on the jeans he looked down at the floor next to the bed and saw the three spent condoms, thick as slugs from the wad of cum inside them. God, he hadn't remembered that. If those fucks had been anything like what the guy had done in the shower . . . Why couldn't he remember? He shook his head, zipped up the jeans, and padded out to the living area.

Guess he'll expect a breakfast for his efforts, Clint thought as he moved into the kitchen area and opened the refrigerator. Not knowing what they'd done earlier, he'd been prepared to send the guy on his way—in fact, he'd already tried that. But after knowing now what the guy could do, the dude at least deserved breakfast.

He took a carton of eggs out of the refrigerator, extracted three, put them in a bowl, and returned the carton to the shelf. He scrounged around in the refrigerator and came up with some cheese and butter, a carton of milk, and mushroom slices. He'd make them an omelet. He was going over in his mind how to get that done as he started the coffee going.

Swinging up from under the counter with a frying pan, his attention was arrested by the black guy standing in the bedroom door, leaning up against the door frame—posing for him, naked and smiling knowingly. Knowing he was hung and cut and knowing that he had fucked Clint thoroughly, putting some meaning behind that "You're all mine now" comment. Declaring with the open ease of his stance that he had marked territory.

Clint took one look at what was swinging between the guy's legs and remembered how hard and long the guy had taken him in the shower, the second time harder than the first, the two of them moving against each other just like long-time lovers. They had wound up sideways in the stall, with Clint's feet leverage off the glass shower stall sliding door and the two pounding against each other to get the black guy as deep inside him as possible in a

20

rapid-fire pumping. And Clint had been impressed at how the guy's muscles bulged in the effort and how much grunting he could do in the process. Near the end, Clint had just collapsed in ejaculation and exhaustion, and the black guy had turned him on his cock, Clint held in front of him like a loose rag doll, his feet and arms dangling, and the black guy had finished him by gripping his waist and slamming him back and forth on his cock. Clint begging for mercy but not wanting any; both of them knowing he didn't.

Three eggs wouldn't do for that performance. He opened the refrigerator again and took out two more. Then he began breaking them against the side of the bowl and letting the contents slip into the bowl while butter sizzled in the frying pan.

"Fixin' somethin' to eat?"

Were all of this guy's brains in his balls? This was the second dumb question he'd asked, and the guy was the silent type. He hadn't said much else other than that. But he cocked so well, Clint would be forgiving.

"Breakfast. I figured we both could use that before we both shoved off—in our separate directions." The guy was good. Well, better than good. But he wasn't anything permanent. Clint wasn't taking any of this "You're mine now" crap.

"Breakfast? It's three in the afternoon. But, yeah, I could use some grub. After that, it's back in the bedroom. I haven't finished balling you good yet. You're one of the best pieces I've ever had."

"Three in the afternoon?" Clint asked, shocked. The sun had been shining, but it came up early this time of year. "What happened to the morning? And why are you even here?"

"I'm here because you wanted to be fucked. Couldn't get enough of me. Blew me as soon as you got in the truck and then begged me to ball you. Didn't have any rubbers on me, so you said we should come here."

"I . . . I don't remember any of that."

"Maybe not—at least fully. You acted like you were on drugs. But you sure remember my cock, I'll bet."

Yeah, Clint did, but only as long ago as the shower. The drugs reference rang a bell, though. He'd been in the back of the limo with the Sicilian guy and his driver. And they'd been using

21

poppers on him while they worked him over good, wanting him to be awake for it.

"Where was this you picked me up?"

"Out on Long Island, next to a cemetery. You were stumbling down the road, just in briefs, with the rest of your clothes under your arm. Don't you remember this?"

"Vaguely. It's coming back. And you stopped for me?"

"Yeah, and you wanted to give a blow job right off. And then you wanted to be fucked, but you kept saying you wanted me to take you home because we needed rubbers. Good thing we did; I don't carry around enough to satisfy you. Listen. You ain't gonna say you didn't want to do this, are you? You ain't sayin' you don't want me to take you back into the bedroom and stuff you good after we eat?"

"It's three in the afternoon. I've got to get to work. You've probably got to get to work too." Then Clint remembered that he'd been told to take the whole day off because they'd worked through the night looking for the body that had been found in the New Jersey landfill.

"Yeah, yeah, I want you to fuck me again after we eat. But then I've got to get to work."

"To work after a couple of hours?—'cause if I get to start fuckin' you again, it ain't gonna be in cut time—and I like to do doubles. What kinda work do you do?"

"I'm a cop. A homicide cop."

If a black guy could blanch, this one did. But Clint didn't see him do it. He was working on getting the omelet set and not burned. When he looked up the guy had already returned to the bedroom, quickly pulled on his jeans, black athletic T, and sneakers, and then, in a silent flash, the door from the living room to the outside hall was hanging open.

Seeing that he was alone, Clint looked down at the five-egg omelet and wondered how he was going to eat all of that himself.

"Shit, he never even gave me a name." And then he thought, because he couldn't bear to say it out loud. I'm such a slut. I blew him and he fucked me who knows how many times and I don't even know who he is. And, fuck, I'm already mad that

22

he's not going to fuck me again after I eat this—or at least try to eat all of this.

* * * *

"Thought you were sleeping this day out."

The first one—practically the only one—Clint saw when he walked into the squad room was Danny Thompson, his most-of-the-time partner and his off-and-on-again lover. Danny was black and a big bruiser, and it wasn't until Clint walked into the squad room that he realized that it had been Danny he'd been associating the black guy in his apartment this morning with. If anyone alive could be said to have marked his territory with Clint, it was Danny. Pairing the black guy in his apartment with Danny, who he closely resembled, had probably been why Clint hadn't been set off by finding a man in his bed when he woke up.

That thought gave Clint some comfort. He'd been berating himself all the time he was eating that five-egg omelet that he'd gotten so loose he'd bring a man home with him even when he was semiconscious. He was familiar enough with murder cases in the gay community to know that this wasn't safe behavior.

The squad lieutenant, Burton Kahn, was in his office too. But then, Kahn always seemed to be on duty. Danny had been returning from a vacation out of town the previous day, so he hadn't been out on the street all night like the rest of them were. So he was at work, while most of the rest from the Special Homicide Unit were off catching up on their sleep. That's what the police squad Clint worked for was called—the Special Homicide Unit. But he was in even a smaller squad of that. The special unit combined Vice cops with Homicide cops because so much of the crime in New York city was sex-based. But Clint and Danny's little unit was more specialized than that. They were assigned to gay male homicides. And to help in the investigations of these—to let the cops go where they needed to go and do what they sometimes needed to do to get the bad guy—all of the guys except for the lieutenant, Burton Kahn, were gay themselves.

Danny and Clint had been lovers for some time, starting shortly after Clint had been assigned to the unit. Danny was the forceful kind. Already knowing Clint was gay and a bottom, he just cornered Clint one day in a room in the tombs and fucked the wadding out of him. Like the guy from earlier today, he'd made it clear he was marking his territory with Clint, making sure all of the other guys in the squad knew that he had. Clint liked it that way, so they'd melded, and the other guys had kept away, some more willingly than others. They'd even commandeered that room in the tombs so that Danny could conveniently relieve Clint's need for sex.

But then along came Brad Roberts from Vice in a combined operation, and Clint was hooked. Brad was handsome and all finesse. He too showed Clint who was boss from the beginning, meeting him in a club in Chelsea, paying the cover, ordering the drinks, and, after paying the tab, just telling Clint they would go back to his place, where he fucked Clint three ways from Sunday on his queen-sized bed, on the thirty-fourth floor in front of a full-wall glass window with a panoramic view of the city.

It turned out that Brad—secretly—was as rich as Clint was, also secretly. The difference being that Brad had great taste and style and knew how to spend his money. Brad was well trained in the martial arts, and he taught so many things to Clint in the short time they were lovers, quite a few of them sexual positions in which Clint was powerless to Brad's invasion. He knew what to do with Clint even better than Danny did.

Clint moved in with Brad, but they were looking for another place they both would consider they'd picked when, during a combined operation trying to trap a gay mobster with murderous appetites, Brad had become a victim. Clint followed the mobster to Europe, relentlessly pursuing him until Brad's death was revenged. But Clint needed more than revenge to assuage the guilt of having lost Brad and having, he thought, permitted him to be lost.

Danny, who had not given Clint up to Brad quietly or willingly, swept back into Clint's life. Wounded and scarred, Clint hadn't given up full control to Danny the second time as he had the first, so their relationship was a bit rocky now. Strangely, it was at its best when Danny sensed Clint was antsy in his sex life and just hunted him down like a warrior and a stag, jumped his bones, and rode him to the ground with his cock.

"I couldn't sleep," Clint said to Danny. "And we've got this case. It was knocked out for a day by the call to search for that witness' body found in Jersey. With a serial like this, a day goes by without work and it could be another life."

"Couldn't sleep? You need some? You want to go down to the tombs? Or we could go to the break room. No one much is here." Danny was giving Clint, sitting across from him, the backs of their desks pushed together, an intense look. The "some" he was referring to was a fucking, and Clint understood it to be. Danny knew that Clint was a satyriasist, a guy who needed sex almost constantly, and Danny was more than happy to oblige.

"No, I just need to get into some work."

Danny gave him an even closer stare. If Clint was out canvassing the city over the previous day and a half, he would have been a day and a half without getting any. So who had given it to him in the meantime? Clint looked entirely too calm and sleek now not to have been screwed in the last day—and screwed good too. "I called you last night. No one answered."

"When I want sleep I plug in earphones," Clint answered, "listen to waves crashing on the shore. The neighborhood I moved into is too noisy at night without the earphones." He was looking down at papers he was shuffling around on his desk.

Danny didn't like it. If there was a scale for jealousy and possessiveness going up to ten, Danny was like a twelve or thirteen.

"Cruising. You been—?"

"Anything breaking on the Santora case?" Clint broke in.

Danny paused. Clint was being assertive today. So, yeah, he'd been screwed good in the last few hours. But he'd drop that in another couple of hours. Another couple of hours and Danny would be begged to do him. Danny could wait.

"Autopsy should be done. I was just about ready to go to the morgue. You wanna come along."

"Yeah, of course," Clint said, standing up from his desk again.

Dix Santora was a blond stockbroker last seen alive in the Splash bar on 17th Street in Chelsea. The next time he was seen was between two sea containers on the docks below Christopher Street. He'd been beaten to death. He was the third guy found like this in the last five months. It looked like a serial killing case, but there was an irregular length of times between killings, which was a bit odd for a gay male serial. All three were good-looking blonds in their early thirties cruising gay bars for tops. And witnesses were indicating that all three of them liked it a little rough. All three of them certainly had gotten what they got more than a little rough. The first two had been last seen in Christopher Street bars and had had sex before they died. But their bodies had been washed and no fingerprints or DNA had been found. The first two had been beaten badly and the witness hadn't, but the cause of death of all was asphyxiation, possibly by a plastic bag held over their heads while they were being choked. The autopsy on Dix Santora would be determining whether he'd had sex too. The speculation was that perhaps circumstances surrounding the death accounted for why the witness wasn't also beaten; maybe for some reason there hadn't been time for the full routine.

Clint was particularly into this case, as it had been the Splash bar where he'd first hooked up with Brad.

* * * *

"Yes, the same as the others. Anal sex before he died. A bit of swelling, indicating unusual size—that's what determined it was before death. But he was quite active; there's no reason to believe that it wasn't consensual. This time was a rough-sex encounter."

The doctor had raised the sheet so that Clint and Danny could see the victim. He was, as had been reported, quite good looking. And blond. Danny had remarked how similar he looked to Clint—"but not as good looking, of course."

"So, if we get enough leads, you think I could go as bait for an operation on this?"

"Yes, I'm sure you could," Danny answered. "They were all blond lookers of about your age, so appearance might be part of the MO. But you know how I feel—"

"It's part of the job, Danny. It's a big reason they put gay guys in the squad."

Danny didn't say anything. They were both thinking of Brad Roberts. That's what he was doing when he was murdered—

26

by sexual assault. He was being bait in an operation—an operation that didn't get help to him before he was murdered and the killer had vanished. The kicker is that he had gotten ahead of his backup—fatally ahead. And it was exactly Clint's propensity to do the same that had Danny on his tail about participating in such operations. It turned out that the killer of Brad wasn't who they fingered for the murders, but that's who Clint went after, and in running him to ground he'd also uncovered—and brought to justice—the real murderer.

"He's got bruise marks on his ankles and wrists," Clint observed as he looked down at the body of Dix Santora. "He had been bound, I take it?"

"Yes, and before he died."

"So, whatever it was, he didn't take it willingly," Danny said.

"Not necessarily," the medical examiner answered. "The bruising elsewhere, as I said, indicated rough sex. Bondage that left marks could have just been part of the package."

"There's a body on the other table. What case is that?" Clint was anxious to change the subject. This was an overworked discussion between Danny and him. Along with being highly jealous and possessive, Danny also was highly protective, and he'd berated Clint for liking rough sex himself regularly. Clint was having none of that. He'd do his job as fully as any of the other detectives—in fact, because he had failed Brad in his own view, he was willing to take more risks. This too was habitually part of their argument on this topic.

"That's Will Trent. From the mobster trial case," the doctor said. "That's the missing witness who was pulled out of the New Jersey landfill yesterday."

"Can we take a look?" Clint asked.

"If you want. I haven't started on him. I will as soon as you are finished here."

The doctor lifted the sheet. Clint audibly sucked in breath and Danny frowned.

"He's blond and good looking and looks to be in his late twenties or early thirties," Danny said. "Not beat up quite so bad, though. Could he maybe be part of our case—maybe just a coincidence he's connected to the mobster case?"

27

"Or maybe that our case is tied into the mobster case," Clint said under his breath—but both Danny and the doctor heard him, and it was Danny's turn to suck in air this time. "And look, he has bruise marks on his wrists and ankles too."

They stood in silence for a few minutes, processing that similarity between the circumstances of the two corpses.

"Will he be tested for anal sex, Doc?" Danny asked.

"Of course."

"Can you refer your findings to the Special Homicide Unit?"

"Certainly."

* * * *

Clint was drawn to the Splash bar in Chelsea. The reminders today were just too much. Danny had pressed him for a hookup, but Clint said there was a movie he wanted to see—and that he really wanted to be alone this evening. Danny knew that Brad was a touchy subject with Clint and that Brad still existed as a wedge in their relationship, so he didn't press. Clint had already seen the movie, so he was prepared to talk to Danny about it the next day, if Danny asked. And being possessive and a good cop, Danny undoubtedly would work it into the conversation.

Clint didn't really want to be alone. He wanted sex. But he didn't want it from Danny. Danny would be at him again about taking risks and wanting it rough. That's not what he wanted to hear tonight. That would kill the heights of arousal he reached when the sex was dangerous and rough.

No sooner had he settled at the bar of Splash than he was breathing ragged, and hardening up—because he was taking a risk.

The big bruiser was standing at the door of the bar, looking intensely around the place in a sweep that didn't miss a face. Clint had already sensed a couple of guys, either of which was acceptable, circling him, ready to press in.

But the bruiser—the driver from the previous night, the Sicilian's chauffeur and bodyguard and, apparently, gofer—saw him and cut through the crowd to reach him.

"The boss wants you again. The limo's outside."

As soon as Clint had seen the guy at the door of the bar, he realized that he wanted more of what he'd gotten the previous night—from the same guy, the guy this bruiser had called "the boss." He pushed away from the bar, gave an apologetic look in turn to each of the guys who were zeroing in on him—there would be other nights and other opportunities if their paths crossed again—and followed the driver out of the bar.

He was expecting the Sicilian to be in the backseat and that they'd fuck there again, but he wasn't there. They drove for more than an hour.

"I hope I won't just be dumped out somewhere like last—" Clint started to say, striving to strike up some sort of conversation with the silent guy who could at least give some sort of reaction. He'd been interested enough to join in fucking Clint the previous night.

"Shut the fuck up, blondie," the driver growled over his shoulder. "You wanted it rough and you got what you wanted. You're lucky the boss liked what you had to give and wants it again. Otherwise you might have stayed permanently where we dumped you—in a graveyard somewhere."

There wasn't much Clint could say to that. He was hard just at the sound of the driver's growl.

They cruised out of the city and onto Long Island, where the limo stopped in front of tall metal gates in a cushy residential area of large-acreage estates and hilly, forested land. The gates opened for them without the driver getting out of the car. Clint saw two mean-looking guards in camouflage, with machine guns at the rest, on the edge of the drive as they drove in.

The Sicilian's party room was in the basement of a large, Spanish-style house. They entered through a door into the basement in a sunken patio at the side of the house, not directly into the main house. Two more armed guards stood on the walls above the sunken patio. Clint ruminated on how big an army it would take to get at the Sicilian in this compound—and hoped that it would be as easy for him to get out as it was being for him to get in.

At first appearances the room looked like it was a gym. All sorts of fancy equipment that looked like it was for exercising. But Clint quickly could see that the equipment was for sexual pleasure, not for exercising—although some of it looked like it would give the receiver a total workout.

The Sicilian already was there when Clint and the driver arrived. So too was the blond bartender from The Dugout, Greg.

The Sicilian—naked and looking massive, hairy, and dangerous—was carrying a drooping Greg across the floor. Clint had no idea what apparatus Greg had been on, but whichever one it was, it looked like it's use had drained the fight from him. He too was naked. And in this light he looked slightly older than he had in the bar. It wasn't lost on Clint that he looked like he was in his early thirties, that he was blond, and that he was very, very good looking. Clint's detective antennae went rigid. However, so had his cock. This was exactly the sort of danger and risk he'd been looking for when he came out to the bars this evening.

He couldn't help himself. He wanted what he knew was coming.

In the brief moment Clint had stood there, taking the room and its occupants in, the driver had stripped. The Sicilian handed Greg off to the driver. Greg didn't seem to like the transfer and was wiggling around in the driver's arms. The driver manhandled him over to the side of a padded platform, lowered Greg's feet to the floor, and pulled Greg's buttocks into his crotch. Clint saw him lift Greg's body so that his hardening cock went between the blond bartender's thighs. What he saw that was surprising, though, was that the driver brought an arm around and palmed Greg's belly. The transformation was immediate and dramatic. Clint heard Greg moan and lift one arm to encircle the driver's neck. He turned and raised his face and their lips met. He also arched his back and lifted his buttocks. His free hand went to under his ball sack and he was helping the driver position his cock at his hole and pretty much climbed on and swallowed the cock in his channel.

The driver pushed the blond's torso down on the top of the padded platform and, maintaining his palming of Greg's belly, began to pump him. Greg was moaning and docilely taking the cock.

"Erogenous zone. We found the young man's erogenous zone," the Sicilian said in the way of explanation, having noticed

Clint's perplexed look. "Do you have an erogenous zone too, Mr. Movie Star? If you do, we'll find it, even if you try to hide it."

"Just about anywhere you want to lay your hands," Clint answered.

The Sicilian laughed. "Have you ever been fucked in a sling?"

"Yes, of course."

Clint had, but he hadn't been fucked often with his legs and arms running up the suspension chains and cuffed tightly while his oppressor used various dildos and graduated-sized beaded and balled strings inside him before fucking him hard.

"The session must be short, I'm sorry to say," the Sicilian said after he'd ejaculated. "Our other guest has agreed to stay the night and I would like another crack at him before Jocko uses him all up. Perhaps you will come for a night soon."

"I can do that, yes," Clint said. "It would be nice I was given a ride back into the city and not just dumped out here, though."

"I have enjoyed you and my special guests get special service," the Sicilian answered. "Like this."

Clint hadn't noticed the Sicilian picking up the metal rod. But he felt it go into his ass, and when the Sicilian turned on the electricity, he screamed and his body lifted off the sling. His come shot straight up out of his erect shaft. The Sicilian laughed.

The driver dropped him off two blocks from his apartment. Clint had given him a false address—but one close enough for him to hobble home. He wanted the ride, but he didn't want the Sicilian to know precisely where he lived.

Once more he was completely satisfied sexually. The Sicilian had done things to him he'd never experienced before— and promised that there was more they could explore. His channel was still tingling from the electric prod. But his ankles and wrists were sore.

Hmm, he thought, as he pushed up the sleeve of his shirt. Bruise marks just like those that were on the bodies of the two men in the morgue.

Chapter Three: Three Cases or One?

Clint arrived at work the next morning as the lieutenant was gathering the squad around the case board, which had the photos of three similar-looking blond-headed men—the three victims of the case they were working on—pinned to the center of the board. Another photo of a similar-looking man was pinned off to one side. Clint recognized this one as the dead witness in the mobster trial case. And two more photos of blond-headed men were grouped off to another side of the board. Burton Kahn was still working on the board, writing notes in black marker under the photos. Clint could understand the photo of the witness being given a tentative identification, but who were the two on the other side of the centered photos, he wondered.

He'd been a few minutes late because he'd stopped at a Starbucks down the street and bought two coffees. Everyone in the squad thought the coffee in their own break room as well as that in the cafeteria downstairs was swill, even though that didn't stop them from inhaling it when they were too busy to send someone out to Starbucks.

He put one of the coffees down on the desk Danny Thompson was sitting at, gave him a tentative smile, and then moved, with his own coffee, to the other side of those gathered. One of the older and more senior detectives, Neil Paxton, was standing behind a lectern next to Kahn. He was the squad's lead investigator, and Clint presumed he was the one who would brief them on the case this morning.

The coffee for Danny was a peace offering, but what it— and the smile—did was put worry and a questioning look on

Danny's face. Clint looked entirely too chipper. To Danny, that could only mean one thing. There had been three voicemail messages from Danny on Clint's cell phone when Clint had checked it at breakfast this morning. He'd had the phone turned off from the time he'd entered the Splash bar and when he'd dragged out of bed, showered, and reached the breakfast table. Danny would know that he didn't just go to a movie last night. And from the progressively high decibel ratings of the phone calls from Danny, he obviously had been pissed when Clint wasn't picking up.

Clint knew the coffee was no better than a stopgap peace offering—letting Danny know that Clint wasn't avoiding him because he was pissed with Danny. But Clint also knew that Danny would want a piece of him sooner than later and would assume that Clint would need the fuck too if he wasn't getting more than enough from somewhere else. The trouble with that was that the Sicilian and his driver were giving Clint more than enough—and Clint wasn't ready to stop seeing them.

Clint tried another smile for Danny from across the room and mouthed a "later." That seemed to bring Danny's "seethe" level down enough for him to visibly relax and turn his attention to the case board. Danny's change of perspective drew Clint also to look at the board. He gasped—loud enough for the two guys he was sitting next to to turn with questioning looks. He just shook his head, suggesting nothing was wrong. But something was terribly, terribly wrong.

Burton Kahn had just put up another head-shot photo next to that of the mobster case witness victim. It was a photo of the Sicilian who had been balling Clint.

Clint sat in a daze as Neil Paxton quieted the guys down.

"It's possible in the time we were pulled to search for the body of the mobster case witness, Will Trent, that our case has expanded," Paxton said in a booming voice. "As you can see, Lieutenant Kahn has put more photographs up on the case board, and as you can also see, most of these men share traits—all except for this photo of Marko Brunelli, the mobster, Burton has just put up beside that of Trent. Brunelli is the mobster in the case Trent was supposed to be testifying in. He's in court this afternoon again, where the judge will decide whether Trent's death means there's a mistrial."

"Yeah, but what does that have to do with our case?" asked one of the detectives. "They found the body, so we're off that gig."

"There are similarities in the Trent death and those in our case, it appears—beyond their appearances. The medical report shows he had bruises on his ankles and wrists, just as the victims in our cases did—and that he'd had anal sex before he died."

"So?" Danny asked. "He was found in a New Jersey dump, and there's every reason to believe he was killed as part of this mobster trial. The others were connected with the docks before they died."

Clint was still in a half daze. He was keeping his head down, not wanting to take another look at the photograph, not wanting to be sure that the man he'd been with the last two days was the mobster, Marko Brunelli. The reference to the bruised wrists and ankles cut through the haze, though, and he involuntarily pulled his sleeves down to cover the bruises on his wrists—the bruises that Marko Brunelli had caused the previous night by cuffing him to the sling in his basement and then doing things to him that made him writhe and pull at the bindings.

"We now know that the last place Trent was seen on the night he was murdered was a bar, The Dugout, on Christopher Street," Paxton answered. "That street runs down the center of Manhattan and into the docks area."

Clint winced again. The Dugout was the bar where he'd first hooked up with Brunelli.

"And beyond that," Paxton continued, "we'd really, really like to like Brunelli for all of these killings. We've been wanting to put him away permanently for more years than most of us have been on the force."

"At this time, and because of where we are in the briefing," Burton Kahn spoke up, "I'd like to introduce Assistant D.A. Henry Hodgkins. There in the back of the room."

All heads swiveled to the back of the room, where a tall man in his forties and wearing a well-cut pin-striped power suit was leaning against of the frame of the door leading out into the corridor. His arms were crossed on his barrel chest, and he was looking like he owned the room. He nodded toward the lectern to acknowledge the shout out, but Clint felt like the man was staring straight at him—just as if he knew everything about how Clint was unknowingly getting tangled up in this case.

"Because of the Brunelli angle, the D.A.'s office is taking a close interest in our case—and the Trent murder case has been turned over to us. Since Trent was last seen at a gay bar and since he had anal sex before he died—and the coroner indicates he was accustomed to having anal sex—it's natural for us to be included in the case. But there is interest beyond that in the possibility that Brunelli can now be connected to our serial killer case. They would really like that. So, Mr. Hodgkins is going to be consulting closely with us during the investigation."

"More like sticking his nose up our asses," a voice from among the cops muttered. Although muttered, everyone in the room heard it. Kahn glowered in the general direction the voice had come from, and Clint was sure that it was Danny who had said it. The assistant D.A. at the door, though, acted like nothing had been said.

"Yes, well, is that clear with everyone?" Paxton quickly interjected. "If there aren't any questions on that, we can move on to those two other photos on the board."

This successfully deflated the tension in the room, because nearly everyone had been curious about those other two photographs since they'd seen they'd been added to the board within the last day. Clint was still ruminating over the appearance of Brunelli's photograph, but he too was curious enough to half listen to Paxton.

"While you ladies were out strolling the city the other day, I was working the case here," Paxton said. "I did some tooling around on the Interpol site, and I came up with two more murder cases that look very familiar. That's the two guys in the photos. As you can see, pretty boys who are blond, one in his late twenties and the other in his early thirties. I found that they were gay too."

"Murdered where?" The voice from the crowd was Danny's.

"Bermuda," Paxton answered. "And you know the problem we'd seen in the pattern of these other killings—that they didn't follow what would be normal for the type of serial killer we were looking for?"

"That the periodicity was off?" another voice from the room asked.

"Yeah. The victims are so similar that we expected pretty even spacing in the murders," Paxton said. "Well, in my research with the help of the Bermuda police, these two deaths fill the holes we were seeing nicely—other than the Trent death. That still doesn't follow a pattern."

"Anything else tying them together?" Danny asked.

"Yes," Paxton answered. "Those two had last been seen at gay bars near the freighter docks in Hamilton, Bermuda. And with a little more research with the Hamilton authorities, we came up with a freighter that regularly plies between New York and Bermuda carrying foodstuffs Bermuda has to have shipped in. It's Greek registered, but we haven't tracked down who actually owns it yet. It was in the appropriate port during each of the murders. So, we have a job looking at the crew of that freighter, I think."

"That don't tie the murders in with Brunelli too good, though, does it?" Another unidentified voice from the crowd.

"No," Paxton said with an audible sigh. "Or maybe not. We don't know where Brunelli was on those dates yet—and we don't know who owns and operates the freighter yet. So, we have to pin that down. But we're not looking for dissimilarities between the cases right now. As long as we can keep the crimes as possibly linked, the more muscle the brass will let us apply to Brunelli. And we need all the support we can get to pin the witness murder on him."

"We need due diligence and every base covered here, team," Lieutenant Kahn broke in to say, doing what he could to water down what Paxton had said that his supervisors would prefer being left unsaid. "We don't want to make too many assumptions about anything or to do anything that artificially pushes this to one scenario rather than another. That's why we have the photos grouped as they are on this board rather than all together. Neil's already handed out some assignments while we were setting up. He'll connect with the rest of you. It's time now to go out and find out who the bad guy is—or guys."

In the raucous dance that followed as the detectives swirled around the room settling into their assignments or grabbing their gear and heading for the door, Danny descended on Clint, who was still sitting there, trying to recover from the shocking discovery that had landed him, unwittingly, in the shit. Kahn had told him on more than one occasion that he needed to rein in his cruising behavior—that someday it would come back to bite him in the ass if it didn't get him killed. And today appeared to be that day.

"Whatsa matter with you, Clint?" Danny was asking. "You look like your get up and go just got up and went."

"Uh, it's nothing, Danny. Maybe a bad egg or something for breakfast." Ha, he thought, he'd had no eggs for breakfast. He'd used them all the previous day to feed a black stud who had just disappeared on him without a word or anything before he'd eaten the eggs—just took a powder when he learned Clint was a cop. Clint hadn't even bothered to find out who he was. He could be a serial killer too, as far as Clint would have known.

"Paxton's told me to put in an appearance at Brunelli's trial this morning. You wanna come with? We need to know if the judge is going to call a mistrial and let Brunelli loose. Not that Brunelli's been in custody, I'll bet. With the fancy-dancy lawyer like he's probably got, I'm sure Brunelli's been out on bail and wasn't even told he shouldn't be popping off prosecution witnesses."

"No, he's not," Clint murmured.

"No, he's not what, Clint?"

Clint clenched his jaw. He couldn't confirm that Brunelli wasn't in custody without revealing why he knew that.

"You're lookin' needy to me," Danny continued. "You goin' with me or does Paxton have you doin' somethin' else? If you're goin' with me, maybe we need to take a side trip to the tombs first. You look like you're needing some."

"Yeah, I'll go with you, but we should talk first. You've got to know something first."

"Yeah what?"

"I know that Brunelli guy. I just didn't know he was Brunelli. That last couple of nights—"

"You hooked up with that Brunelli guy, and you're lettin' him ball you, is that what you're gonna say? That's where you've been the last two nights?" Danny hadn't been quiet when he'd said this. Both Clint and Danny reflexively looked around the room to see if anyone heard that. Apparently they hadn't; the noise level was high and everyone was jabbering with someone else. After they'd checked, Danny grabbed Clint's shirt front in a fist and brought their faces close together. "Jesus H. Christ, Clint. You're gonna get yourself killed lookin' for it that rough."

"He didn't have an 'I am a mobster' button pinned to his shoulder, Danny. Maybe we'd better go to the tombs and discuss this." Clint pushed Danny's hand away.

The two had a room they used during the day when the manning level of the precinct offices was high. There were a series of interview rooms down in the basement. Some were better appointed than others, because the budget hadn't allowed for them all to be brought up to state of the art. So, there were a couple that never were used. The unused ones had just been locked up awaiting the day when a line item mysteriously appeared in the police budget to renovate them. Danny had the key to one of the unused rooms. There was a window in the door, of course, and a one-way glass permitting observation from another room, but both had been papered over, and no one had bothered to take the paper off. The only item of furniture in the room was a wooden table, and there were hooks on the wall for them to hang their clothes. And that was all that Danny and Clint needed. An emergency supply of Danny's favorite ribbed maxim condoms was kept in a drawer in the table.

Danny hustled Clint down the three flights to the tombs and down the corridor to "their" room. Once in and the door locked behind them, Danny propelled Clint to the table and pushed him down on his butt on the table top.

"Danny, we got to talk about this."

"Damn right we gotta talk this," Danny growled, pulling the drawer in the table open. "But you want it rough. You like a rough guy. OK, you got a rough guy."

He pushed his knees between Clint's thighs.

"Danny," Clint said, raising his torso from the table top.

38

Danny backhanded him across the cheek and Clint fell back onto the table, hitting his head, momentarily dazed. Danny had both of their cocks out and fisted together and he was pulling on them.

"Danny, Danny," Clint murmured. He made a weak attempt to rise again, but Danny just pushed his back down on the table again with the palm of the hand he wasn't stroking with palmed on Clint's sternum. Lost to the stroking, Clint lay there and moaned. Visions of that blond guy, Greg, in Brunelli's basement the previous night and how he'd gone docile when the mobster's driver palmed his belly floated into his mind. He'd told Brunelli that he had erogenous zones too. And Danny knew that. He knew that all anyone had to do was to get Clint's cock in their hand, and Clint wanted to be fucked.

He just lay there, moaning and saying, "We've got to talk this, we've got to talk this," as Danny stripped off his trousers and briefs, fished a small tube of lube out of the table drawer, and opened the condom packet with his teeth.

Clint's talk of the need to talk turned into murmurs of what he wanted more of, deeper and faster, as Danny buried his cock inside him and started to pump. Clint arched his back, hooked his ankles above Danny's buttocks, and panted as Danny fucked him to a mutual ejaculation.

"Now, do we need to go tell Lieutenant Kahn that you've been fucking our primary suspect?" Danny asked through his own breathing when they were done. He was still buried inside Clint and his chest was propped above Clint's torso by fists pressed into the table top on either side of Clint's biceps.

"He'll have me reassigned—best scenario—I won't be able to work the case. We won't be able to work it together. Is that what you want, Danny?"

Danny's expression turned to a more thoughtful one than he'd been exhibiting before he'd gotten Clint fucked.

"So, you won't be able to go to the court room with me?" Danny said, assuring Clint that he'd played a trump card. Danny couldn't give him up. "He'll see you."

"There are those rooms at the back with the one-way glass," Clint said. Danny was still in the saddle and Clint was unbuttoning his shirt and running his hands up Danny's massive chest. "I've got to go. I have to be sure it's him."

"He'd be turned to the front and might be too interested in the proceedings to do much looking around in the crowd. Maybe if you just sat slouched down in the back . . . stop that; you're making me hard again."

"I want you hard again. He's got a bodyguard and driver who would probably be sitting in the crowd," Clint answered.

"The bodyguard's been fucking you too?"

Clint didn't answer. He was thumbing Danny's nipples and Danny was breathing heavily, and they both could feel him going harder inside Clint.

"Christ almighty, Clint. You're a regular fuckin' bunny, aren't you?" He tried to make it sound gruff, but how Clint was was a turn on for Danny too. Whenever he could smell another man on Clint, he got harder and fucked longer.

"Danny!" Clint cried out and arched his back and grabbed Danny's waist with his hands. But Danny already was starting to pump hard and deep again.

* * * *

"OK, you've now seen him and confirmed it's Brunelli who's been balling you. You're going to just drop it now, right? You aren't going to see him again."

Clint could tell that Danny had been building up to saying something, and when it finally came out, he wasn't that surprised what Danny wanted to establish. But he didn't answer immediately. They were both still processing what they had just observed.

They were in the glassed-off room at the back of the courtroom, which was clearing. The judge in the case had surprised—and angered—everyone in the courtroom equally. On the one hand, He hadn't thrown the case out. He was allowing the prosecution to go on, even in its wounded condition from being down one key witness. That had set Brunelli off enough that he'd cursed the judge loudly and shaken his fist at him. The outburst had been such a surprise that everyone in the room was trying to remember if the curse contained a threat as well—but no one could be sure that it had.

Conversely, the prosecutor had almost done the same when the judge just ignored Brunelli's outburst and had failed to either revoke or stiffen his bail. Clint had seen that the assistant D.A. from the morning's squad briefing, Henry Hodgkins, was just sitting at the prosecution table, cool as a cucumber and looking relaxed through the commotion, but the D.A. himself had reddened right up at Brunelli being left free in the face of the murder of a key witness against him and had huffed and puffed until the judge had stared him down and banged his gavel before getting up and leaving the courtroom.

"He found me—both times—Danny. I didn't go looking for him."

"But he found you in the same bars the victims in our case disappeared from, didn't he? You've been cruising the bars near the docks—the rough trade bars."

"They aren't all rough trade, Danny."

"But it's rough trade you've been looking for, isn't it? And you are failing to connect the dots. I swear, Clint, that your 'gotta have it rough all the time' is a blind spot to your investigation abilities."

"You know me Danny. And we both know my 'gotta have it' plays right into your own interests."

"Well, you should just take your cruising up town for a while—until we nail this guy for something."

"You don't mean that, Danny. You don't want me cruising for it at all. Admit it."

Danny didn't admit. He just set his jaw and looked stubborn.

Seeing that this was going nowhere, Clint changed direction. "It could be a good thing that I might get close to him again, Danny. It's the perfect setup. I'd be on the inside and we wouldn't even have to plan a way for one of us to get on the inside."

Danny's stubbornness wasn't ready to let loose. "Him being a mobster—and murderer—excites you, doesn't it, Clint? If he comes for you again, you'll go, won't you?"

Clint didn't answer. Danny knew him too well. He knew that this all made the mobster more arousing to Clint, not less.

The courtroom had cleared and they were walking out to the lobby. Hodgkins was still there, loitering around, appearing to be waiting for someone. When Hodgkins saw Clint and Danny come into the lobby, Clint could have sworn that the man smiled at him and gave him a wink. The assistant D.A. turned and left the building then, but as he left, Clint was already imagining what he might look like undressed.

"Can you at least wear a wire or something—keep a cell phone open—let me know somehow where you are so that we can stay near and know if you need to be pulled out?"

"A wire wouldn't work. You know that, Danny," Clint answered. "You know I wouldn't be wearing anything and that anything on my clothes would be found. But, yes, I think I know that's why I needed to tell someone about Brunelli and me—that I had to tell you. I know that I need backup. But it may all just be spinning wheels. Maybe he's done with me. I don't get the impression that he sticks with one guy too long."

"Yeah. That may be the problem, Clint. Maybe he just fucks them and then beats them to death when he gets bored with them. That might be what our serial killings here are all about. You can only like that up to a point, no matter what greater high you think is out there. What good is a new high if you're too dead to remember it?"

Chapter Four: On the Docks

"It don't look like much of a ship to me."

"It only has to get to Bermuda and back," Clint answered.

He and Danny were standing on the docks below Christopher Street and looking up at the small freighter being loaded with boxes they'd seen were marked with everything from canned goods to dry goods to fresh fruits and vegetables.

Danny walked over to a guy standing near the gangplank who was holding a clipboard and marking off boxes as hulking stevedores wheeled them up the gangplank on dollies. There were cranes working on loading some of the other ships at the dock, but this one apparently didn't merit that attention.

Clint was watching the stevedores work. And a couple of stevedores were giving Clint close scrutiny. He'd seen a couple of them in the Christopher Street bars, he thought. He might even have been fucked by one or more of them in back rooms of the bars.

Focus, he thought, and turned his attention back to Danny and the guy with the clipboard.

"This the Greek ship that makes the run to Bermuda?" Danny asked the guy.

"Yeah, this is the *Larnaka Star*," he answered in a pure New York accent that indicated he may never actually have ever been to Bermuda himself. "It's not Greek, though. The name pegs it as Cypriot, as does that flag up there. Not all that much difference, though. Both are just flag-of-convenience registration states. From the language I've heard coming off this freighter's decks, I'd say it was more East European or Russian."

"So, do you know who owns it?"

"Nah. I can tell you who the supplier is—Falzone Holdings. But I don't know who owns it."

"Sounds like an Italian name—Sicilian even," Clint said, having been drawn over to the conversation.

"I wouldn't know. But what's this interest? If you're the Feds, all the paperwork is in order. And we do this like every two weeks. Nothin's going on here to raise eyebrows. It's just regular weekly supplies out to Bermuda. Places is pretty much a barren rock, you know. Most everything has to be shipped in. Even a lot of drinking water shipped there."

"No, no, nothing questionable about your paperwork," Danny said quickly. "Some of the guys are just thinking of taking a trip to Bermuda. Hitting on the casinos there, you know—and we've heard that freighters sometimes rent cabins to travelers. You know if this one does?"

"If it does, it would be a pretty rough way to get there," the guy with the clipboard answered. He paused to take down the number of a box going up the gangplank. "And if you know where there's a casino in Bermuda, I'd sure like to know where it is. I've been there three times in the last ten years and every time I've been there casinos have been illegal. Take Royal Caribbean. They got casinos right on the ship. But they have to close down when they're in port in Bermuda."

Danny thanked the guy and he and Clint pulled off to the side.

"Heard that? Could be Sicilian, so maybe this Falzone Holdings is a cutout company owned by Brunelli."

"Should we go aboard and see if we can bluff some information from the captain?" Clint answered.

"No. It would probably just shut him down and alert someone of our interest. We want a list of his crew members who would have been in port when the murders happened. And we'd want to know if Brunelli ever used the ship to get to Bermuda. So, we need a search warrant for all their records. I'll go see what I can do about that. You might wander over to the port authority and see if you can get more information on who owns the ship."

"And we'll meet back at the office?"

"Yeah, it will take some time to get the warrant, I'm sure. It will be too late to get this rapped up today."

"But the ship's going to be going back out when it's loaded. It's carrying fresh produce; that can't just sit here very long. Either another murder might happen, or the ship might be gone before we can get back."

"We'll just have to do what we can," Danny answered. "I can't move a judge any faster than he wants to move. But I'll be sure to mention those possibilities to him. And it won't happen until we get a move on, so I suggest we shove off."

Clint stood a moment longer, looking a bit stubborn. Maybe he could shake something loose sooner. All of the activity he'd seen at the freighter was stevedores on the move. Maybe the crew had dispersed to the local bars. They were at the foot of Christopher Street. It would take Danny a lot longer to get a search warrant than it would for him to see if there were any crew members of the *Larnaka Star* nearby he could talk to. He waited for Danny to be out of sight and then he turned to head up Christopher Street. As he passed by a line of large metal containers sitting on the land edge of the dock, a callused hand reached out and gripped his arm above the elbow and pulled him into the darkness between two containers.

"Remember me?" a voice with a thick European accent asked in a hoarse whisper.

"Maybe," Clint responded, not knowing in the shadows between the containers whether he did or not. He was on assignment, though, and not in the mood. "Don't know if I do, but I'm not—"

The man pulled Clint into his chest. "As I remember, you're always ready to go. Don't get scared or anything. I just want to fuck, and the last time we did you said 'any time, any place.'"

It obviously was one of the stevedores. Heavily muscled. He had a strong arm around Clint's waist, pulling him in, and his mouth was searching for and finding Clint's. Clint was still struggling against the man as the stevedore fumbled with his own belt and zipper and then Clint's. He stuffed a beefy hand down from Clint's belly and under the waistband of Clint's trousers and fisted the detective's cock.

45

"Oh, God. Oh shit, yes," Clint muttered, going completely docile, as he pulled his lips away. The man knew how to take control of him. All Clint needed was a hand on his cock. Maybe he had been with this guy more than once before.

Clint felt his trousers and briefs being pushed down his legs. He was turned belly against the side of a metal container, and the stevedore kept a hold on his cock while he positioned his own cock head at Clint's hole. Now Clint remembered him. A double cock ring, one thick, the other not. Clint remembered how they clicked and jangled inside him before—in the back room of a Christopher Street bar. He couldn't remember which one, but he'd gone back for it the next night.

"Yes, I remember you now," Clint whispered.

"And you want me, don't you?"

"Yes, I want you."

He groaned and widened his stance as the cock started its invasion. Not thick, but long, as Clint recalled. And those two cock rings did a job on his channel walls. In the saddle now, the man leaned his beefy chest into Clint's back, pinning him to the wall. He released Clint's cock, that no longer being needed for control, and took Clint's wrists in his hands and forced his arms over his head, Clint's fingers gripping the top edge of the metal container. Clint turned his head back and they went into another kiss. The detective moaned as the cock took a long, clicking slide up inside him. A couple of inches inside him and it drew back. Then he gasped as he felt the slide in, farther this time. Out and in a bit farther.

Clint tore his mouth away to mutter an "Oh fuck, yes. Oh shit yes, I remember this. God, do I remember this" and arched his back and laid his head back on the stevedore's shoulder. He was set for the duration of a good fuck now. He was panting and groaning. The stevedore was groaning too, as the cock slid farther up into Clint's channel and then pulled back. He shuddered and started pumping harder. Click, click, click.

"Shit, shit, shit. FUCK."

"Jorge, where the fuck are you? You just had your break." The deep, irritated voice rang out over the dock area. "Am I gonna have to put a bell on you?"

"Stay here," the man whispered in Clint's ear. "Just about done out there."

And then the stevedore pulled away from Clint's back and out of his channel, pulled his trousers up, and was gone from the shadows into the light of the dock.

Clint waited for a few minutes and then he pulled his briefs and trousers up as well. No way in hell he was going to wait for it here. The guy was gone, so the moment had lost its charm. But now he was horny as hell. He'd be looking for more than information in the Christopher Street bars now. He stumbled out at the other end of the containers from the dockside and started up Christopher Street, thinking on which would be the best one to hit. He decided that the first stop he'd make would be in the basement bar called Chris's in the Christopher Hotel—both gay dives he'd seen sailors from the ships on the dock using. He'd used the rooms in the dump of a hotel himself.

The light was dim in the bar, and it took several moments for Clint to adjust his eyes. The inevitable cigarette smoke didn't help. There wasn't room at the bar and several of the tables were occupied, but Clint saw one just a couple of steps from the bar, and he headed for that. On his way past the bar he signaled the bartender, a butch woman named, surprisingly enough, Chris, for a beer, and she waved her acknowledgment. Clint was no stranger to Chris's—or all that much of a stranger to the rent-by-the-hour rooms in the Christopher hotel above it either. He hadn't been in for a while, though.

He took off his suit jacket and draped it over the chair next to him. He did this to dress down to maybe distinguish himself from most of the others if a sailor from the docks came. Most everyone else in the place was a suited businessman of some sort from the Wall Street district. And if there were going to be sailors here today, they must be coming in later.

"Looks like the place has been upscaled," he said to Chris when she delivered his beer—along with a saucer of peanuts that wouldn't have been provided when he had been here before. He could tell that the place had been painted and new chairs and tables had been brought in too. And there was a platform in the corner with a piano, so they must now feature live music here some time or other.

"New owner," Chris said. "Some sort of hush-hush bigwig, I understand. But his renovations are bringing in better spenders and less riff raff."

"Guess it's outclassed me then," Clint said.

"Nothing outclasses you, doll. With those movie star looks, you always did dress up the place."

When she had returned to the bar, Clint looked around again. There were guys eyeing him from the bar and from the tables as they always did when he came into one of these bars. But their attention was being divided. As his eyes became better adjusted to the low light, he saw that there was another good-looking blond guy, incongruously sporting an abbreviated Mohawk and the same five-O'clock shadow Clint was now cultivating and wearing a trim three-piece suit. Most of the guys in the place had been circling his table when Clint came in, and only some of them were switching to Clint or showing their indecision.

The blond caught Clint's eye and gave him what Clint interpreted as a "No problem; there are enough for both of us" look, and Clint raised his glass. The guy probably didn't like it rough like Clint did and thus was more satisfied with the type of men in here at the moment. Clint needed it now that he'd had a taste. But he'd probably have to wait for later.

But then the composition of the room started to change. Must be closing time on the docks, Clint thought, as more and more rough stevedore and sailor types were coming down the steps into the smoke-filled bar. The Wall Street types were sensing the change in mood and were hooking up and leaving or just leaving. Clint half expected the double-cock ring guy to come in. If he did, Clint was willing to resume their encounter.

Clint noticed a few of the new arrivals moving in on the other blond guy—more aggressively than the Wall Street types had been doing earlier—and he also noticed that the blond guy didn't seem to mind. So, maybe they weren't as different in their tastes as Clint had thought.

"Hey, we meet again. Maybe we start up where we left off again too."

Clint turned, expecting it to be the guy he'd recently left. But it wasn't. He would have asked the new arrival if he wanted to sit down, but he was already sitting. It was the big sailor type with

48

the Russian accent who had evaporated from an advanced move on Clint in The Dugout bar the night Brunelli and his driver had taken him for that first ride.

He quite evidently was from the docks. A good place to start on learning about the crew of the *Larnaka Star*, Clint thought. "Buy me another beer?" he asked. He'd been nursing his and it was down to suds rimming the bottom of the glass.

But the Russian was thinking along a different, faster route. "Been hard for you since the other night. Didn't want to start a fight, but I bet I can do you better than that old punk did." The man was already pushing a knee into Clint's thigh and had a hand on his cock through the material of his suit trousers.

That hand on Clint's cock was pretty much all he needed to do, even if Clint hadn't come in looking for relief as soon as he could get it.

"This place have rooms in the back?" the Russian asked in a thick voice. "Buy you a beer afterward. Then we can go someplace for more fun. But right now—"

"It's a hotel. Their rooms are above us. The back is just a corridor leading to the john and maybe a store room or two."

"Come," The Russian said, standing and pulling Clint up with a firm grasp on his wrist. "I need to piss. So do you."

Clint's eyes surveyed the room again before he let the Russian nudge him toward the back. He could see that the Russian hadn't come in alone. A couple others like him, including the Baltic hulk that had been putting the moves on him at The Dugout along with the Russian, were here and had taken possession of the table where the blond guy with the Mohawk was. Everyone who had been at that table before had cleared away, willingly or not, Clint didn't know. But seeing how bulky and mean-looking the Russian's friends were, Clint assumed the Wall Street types hadn't put up much of a defense.

The Mohawk guy was sitting in the lap of the Russian's friend, who held him in a bear hug. From the expression on the blond's face and the way they were moving in the chair, Clint wondered if there was any trouser material between the two.

The Russian fucked Clint up against the graffiti-covered cinderblock wall half way down the dimly lit corridor from the bar room to the restrooms. He'd knelt in front of Clint, pushing him up against the wall, unbuckled and unzipped him, and pulled his trousers and briefs off him while he was sucking Clint's cock.

"Quick one here, for a taste. Then I really give it to you upstairs," The Russian said as he went downstairs and, with one finger wrapped around the base of Clint's cock, laced his other fingers around Clint's balls and separated, squeezed, and pulled them down away from Clint's groin. Clint rewarded him with a gasp and a groan.

Clint was completely lost as soon as the guy's lips opened over his cock. The Russian had reached up and unbuttoned Clint's dress shirt as he was sucking him and at some point pulled his own T-shirt over his head so that when he rose from the kneeling position and palmed and lifted, spread, and tilted Clint's buttocks into his crotch, their bare torsos were rubbing against each other. He had rings in both of his nipples, and as Clint moaned at the entry of the man's cock into his channel, he realized that the man had a thick cock ring as well. The sensation that this would essentially be an extension of the earlier, disrupted fuck, excited Clint. He hitched his knees on the man's hips and began moving his pelvis in countermotion to the Russian's thrusts.

Men brushed past them going and coming from the restroom, and a few of them paused to watch, but Clint didn't notice them and the Russian obviously didn't care.

All was marching relentlessly to ejaculation when Clint felt the Russian jerking away from him and opened his eyes to see the Russian's head turning to the side in time to meet a fist. The Russian dropped to the floor and Clint would have too, if Brunelli's driver hadn't been quick enough to support his body in a slower slide down the wall.

"You follow the boss here?" he asked in a gruff voice.

"Who? What are you . . . no, I didn't follow anyone here. I come here often. You can ask the woman behind the bar." Clint was suddenly frightened. The last thing he wanted Brunelli to think was that he was following him. No, the *last* thing he wanted Brunelli to find out was that he was a homicide cop and was working Brunelli as a suspect.

"No matter. The boss, he said to bring you upstairs. Put on your pants and let's go." Clint was pulling on his briefs and trousers as he stepped over the prone body of the Russian, who was moaning softly but not necessarily consciously. He was a big man, but he was hunched over, so Clint thought he might have taken a fist to the kidneys at the same time as his nose was readjusted yet again.

Clint was hustled through a door across the corridor that was open now but hadn't been open when the Russian had brought Clint back here. This led into yet another corridor that T'ed into the main one. Two elevators were accessed from this side corridor. One of them had its door open and the manual stop engaged.

Clint had no idea how many floors the elevator rose before it stopped and he was manhandled down the hotel corridor, which had a thug with a machine gun stationed at either end, and shoved through a door and into what was set up as a bedroom. The room was dominated by a four-poster bed. Marko Brunelli was sitting in a wingback chair near a window and drinking a Budweiser beer from a can. He was wearing a business suit and looked pretty spiffy for a chunky, middle-aged mobster.

The first thing he said when the bodyguard had pushed Clint to the center of the room and exited through a side door was just a repeat of what Clint had already heard. "You following me around town and scoping me out, or what?"

"No, as I told your bruiser, I come to Chris's downstairs fairly often. I was in the neighborhood and stopped in for a drink. The bartender knows me. You can ask her." By the time he got to the end of that sentence, Clint could have kicked himself. He hoped he wasn't bringing any trouble to Chris.

"You cruising for men down there?"

"I just came in for a drink."

"But Jocko tells me you found a man, that you was ridin' a man's cock in the hallway."

Jocko. That's what he'd been called before. The bodyguard cum driver's name was Jocko. Clint filed that away in his mind. His mind was actually very good as a file of information that might be useful later.

"He found me. Unfinished business. I don't know him, but I hope he's OK. You play pretty rough."

"And I fuck rough . . . and you like it," Brunelli said. His voice was ice cold, and Clint had no trouble seeing him as someone people feared, tried to steer clear of when they could, and tried to satisfy when they couldn't. "I don't like that you mess around with other men when I'm using you."

Clint didn't know what to say to that that wouldn't bring him trouble, so he said nothing.

"Sit down. The bed's OK. You'll be finding that out," Brunelli said.

Clint sat on the side of the bed. He looked up into the framing at the top of the bed and saw the leads and cuffs at all four corners. He had a feeling he'd been trussed up in those shortly.

"You want a job? Pay would be very good. You'd have a room."

"I have a job," Clint answered. He saw the mistake of saying that as soon as it was out of his mouth. He wanted to keep Brunelli as far away from knowing his job as he could.

"Doin' what?"

"Uh, this and that. Nothing permanent."

"So, I got a job to offer you."

"Doing what?" Clint asked.

"You know what."

"How permanent would that be?"

"That would be up to how long you keep me interested. And speaking of interested." He was putting his beer can down, and Clint didn't have to guess hard what was coming next.

But he was wrong. There was a knock on the door that Jocko had exited and it opened to reveal Jocko filling the space with his hulking figure.

"Your appointment is here, Boss. Should I have him wait over here or downstairs? You gonna make some noise here you don't want him to hear, I can take the guy downstairs till you're done."

"No, no. It's fine. This can wait," Brunelli said, as he rose from his chair and started crossing the room. He gave a "Later" stare to Clint in passing.

When Clint was alone, he let his eyes roam around the room. This wasn't a short-term hotel room. This was set up for long-term occupancy. The furniture was too good and there was too much personal-type stuff sitting around. The bed itself was very expensive looking and was obviously a special piece of equipment. Clint opened the drawers of the nightstand next to where he was sitting and wasn't surprised to find condoms in bulk, lube, and various sex toys.

His attention was arrested by the sound of voices coming from the next room—the room that Brunelli and Jocko had gone into. He realized it probably was a sitting room attached to this bedroom. Clint would check on who had recently bought this hotel and was renovating it, but his vote went to Brunelli.

He could hear Brunelli's fairly high-pitched-voice and a deeper, richer one of another man. There was no question who was in charge and who was trying to please the other one, even though Clint couldn't hear what was said. Brunelli obviously wanted something and wanted it now—and the other man was going to do what he could to make it happen.

After a while, Clint didn't hear the voices anymore. He walked over and put his ear to the door. Nothing. And nothing for a bunch of minutes. He quietly turned the handle of the door and opened it a crack, fully anticipating to feel Jocko's fist come pushing through the opening, but not being able to help himself. Nothing. Opening the door further, he could see that the room, which, as he had surmised was furnished as a setting room—and quite expensively so—was deserted. He clicked the door shut, went to the door from the bedroom to the corridor, and slowly opened that. No one was in the hall.

He took the elevator down to the basement floor. He saw a bit of blood on the main corridor floor where the Russian had been dropped, but no other sign of the sailor. When he entered the bar, however, his eyes opened wide. Danny was sitting at the table he had occupied before the Russian had muscled him into the back. The table was otherwise unoccupied. Clint's suit jacket was on the chair next to Danny. Danny gestured him to the table.

"How did you know I'd be here?" Clint asked as he took a seat. He looked around the room, but there was no Russian. The Wall Street clientele had also turned over completely to something rough this late in the day.

"I followed you here—after your little escapade at the docks." The way Danny said that, clued Clint that he wasn't wild about Clint's little encounter with the stevedore. "I knew you were up to something. I saw you and those stevedores eyeing each other. When I got here, Chris told me you'd gone to the back, so I've been sittin' here, waiting for you. I was about to go exploring for you, though. What gives?"

"Brunelli picked me up here," Clint answered. "I was going to see if maybe there were any crew members of the *Larnaka Star* cruising around here before I went over to the port authority. That wasn't going to take long."

"And yet you didn't get to the port authority."

"No I didn't. But I found out something very useful, I think."

"And I didn't get the search warrant. We'll have to do that . . . you say you found out something useful?"

"Brunelli has a hidey hole here. And he wants to hire me. I can be close to him until we find out what we need to know. I think that's two useful pieces of information."

Danny whistled. "OK, you win. That's two very useful pieces of information indeed."

"But for now, we'd better clear out of here," Clint said. "I wouldn't want Brunelli or his driver to see us together—in case they saw you in the courtroom."

"OK. Your place or mine, then?"

Clint gave Danny a questioning look.

"You don't have that finished look about you," Danny said. "You gonna let me polish you off, or are you going to go back to cruising as soon as we part ways?"

"I don't think I need to answer to you on that."

"Right. My place then. It's closer."

Chapter Five: Did He or Didn't He?

Clint, Danny, and a small team of police officers stood dockside at the foot of Christopher Street and stared morosely at the empty boat slip. The *Larnaka Star* had sailed during the night. Danny had insisted that Clint spend the night with him—and in his bed—and once they'd gotten into work they'd spent the better part of the morning obtaining a search warrant—specifically for the *Larnaka Star*'s crew records for sailings of that past six months. And, having obtained that warrant at last, Danny stood, holding it in his hand and facing an empty slip.

"It's OK, Danny. The freighter will be back in a few days. The search warrant doesn't have to be used today."

Danny turned and gave Clint a sour look. "Yeah, but if we'd had the warrant yesterday, we'd be ahead in this investigation by those days. And there's always a chance we could have saved another life."

"We don't know that, and it was already too late in the day yesterday to get a warrant and exercise it. Come on, we're down here anyway. Let's check out the ownership at the port authority before going back to the precinct."

They dismissed the police search team, with thanks, and went on to the port authority building, where they learned that the ship was owned and operated by a Ukrainian company. There was no hint that Brunelli had a hand in it.

The squad room was astir when they got back, with detectives on the phone and other detectives in serious conversations over maps and such on desktops. The atmosphere was heavy and quite serious. Clint noticed a new photo had been put up in the center of the case board. He went up and looked at it. Another blond guy. Good looking under those facial bruises. But quite clearly dead. He looked familiar and Clint was still trying to place him when Burton Kahn, Neil Paxton, and the assistant D.A., Henry Hodgkins, entered from Kahn's office and Kahn started calling the squad to attention.

As the detectives were settling, Kahn called out to Danny. "The ship?"

"Sailed already. Around 4:00 a.m. this morning, according to the port authority," Danny answered. "The ship's owned by a Ukrainian company; we'll have to get to it when it gets back from Bermuda. Seven days, according to the port authority's records. But what's going down here, Lieutenant."

"We're getting to that," Kahn answered. "Pipe down, folks. Neil will give report."

Neil Paxton moved behind the lectern next to the board. "As you can all see, there's another photo up on the board. Another body found shortly after 10:00 a.m. this morning. Another blond guy in his early thirties. Messed with and beaten up, just like the others. Same bruising to the wrists and ankles, so he'd been bound. Maybe even killed by asphyxiation—possibly a plastic bag over his head, although one wasn't found at the scene. According to what was found in his wallet, his name was Ted Luscum. A trader on Wall Street. No cash was found, but there were credit cards. So, whoever it is is being very careful. We could trace the cards; we can't the cash."

"How long dead?" Danny asked.

"Not more than twelve hours, the medical examiner estimates," Paxton answered. "As usual, he doesn't want to be pinned down on that until he's done an autopsy. Doesn't want to comment on whether the guy was gay or not yet, but he did say he'd had anal sex before he died and, uh, from the size of his asshole, he probably was a frequent taker—but that he'd been cleaned up, so there's not much chance of DNA. The team's still over there, though, trying to find something."

"Over where?" a voice from the crowd asked. "Found near the docks like the others?"

"Close enough to want to lump this murder with the others," Paxton answered. "He was found in a room of the

Christopher Hotel on Christopher Street, yes, down near the docks."

Clint's blood ran cold. He'd just been in the Christopher Hotel. And then it hit him where he'd seen the man in that photo before. It had been just the previous day. That had been the blond guy in Chris's who was sharing the attention Clint had been getting. Clint had been in the same room with him—in a hotel that Marko Brunelli probably owned and where Brunelli had been too—the same day the victim had been there. He was about to pipe up and say something when Kahn started to speak at the lectern again.

"At this point, Assistant D.A. Hodgkins wants to say something."

Hodgkins came to the lectern and began talking, "As you know, this is the fourth similar murder in the New York docks area. The D.A.'s office is going to have to make some sort of statement on these murders and . . ."

Clint didn't hear the rest of what he was saying. He was beginning to hyperventilate. It was a good thing he hadn't had the opportunity to speak up about seeing the victim at Chris's the day before. He'd have to try to sit here, looking calm and sitting on his patience, until this was over and he could speak to Kahn in private.

It was over an hour before he was able to do that, until Hodgkins was gone and the squad had divvied up assignments. Paxton was off to call the Bermuda authorities to tell them there had been another murder and that a crew member of the *Larnaka Star* might be involved—and to request that they keep a surveillance on the freighter but not to do anything until the ship could return to New York where the search warrant could be served on its crew records and schedules and interviews of the crew members could commence.

Danny had gone to the morgue to see if the medical examiner had any more information on the victim that could help him.

"I was at the Christopher Hotel yesterday, Lieutenant. At Chris's, the bar in the basement. You can check with the bartender. She knows me. I was checking there and other bars on Christopher Street to see if I could track down any of the crew members of the *Larnaka Star*. I didn't, by the way. The latest victim, Luscum, was in the bar. And he looked like he was cruising. So, that's a place we can start doing a timeline on him."

"OK, good, thanks for the information, Clint. Is that all? You asked for a private meeting. You could have said all of this while everyone was still together. It's information all of the detectives should know."

"No, that's not all, Lieutenant. I was starting at the Christopher because I understand that Marko Brunelli recently bought the hotel—and we're looking for links between him and these murders. And . . . and I saw Brunelli in the hotel yesterday too."

Clint was moving onto very shaky ground. What if Kahn asked him where, specifically, he'd seen Brunelli? Clint wasn't ready to open up to anyone but Danny on how deeply he was embroiled in this—and he wasn't telling Danny everything yet either. But Kahn didn't go there.

"That would have been good to bring up in the briefing too. But how do you know Brunelli owns the hotel?"

"I'm not certain he does. But that's what my informants down there tell me. I was trying to check that out, because these informants aren't the best. I wasn't going to mention it until it was firmer information. But with another homicide in that hotel . . ."

"OK, that's enough to rattle his cage a bit on this. We'll bring him in for a talk and to let him know we're on the trail. If this is his work, it might at least get him to stop doing it until we can catch up with him. So, is that all?"

"No, Lieutenant, that's not all. Got something very delicate and I can't get into where I've picked it up, but I just need to pass on a warning and a caution on just how much you want to share with this assistant D.A. guy, Hodgkins."

"What are you telling me without telling me?"

"I have some indication that he may be in bed with Brunelli. I'll let you work that out as you see fit. But I've got it from a pretty reliable source—more reliable than the sources on Brunelli owning the hotel. He may be working us from the inside for Brunelli."

Clint had to pass on just enough for Kahn to be careful what he shared with Hodgkins and to put out his own feelers on a possible Hodgkins-Brunelli connection. For Clint's part, he considered his source highly reliable. It was he himself. The voice he'd heard through the hotel room door talking to Marko Brunelli the previous afternoon at the Christopher. It had been Henry Hodgkins. He was sure of it; the man's voice was quite distinctive.

He was about to leave Kahn's office when Paxton poked his head in the door.

"Strangest thing, Burton," he said. "I got through to Bermuda and they already had the *Larnaka Star* on a watch list. But they say that freighter isn't headed to Bermuda this week. No scheduled arrival there this week."

Kahn looked pensive. "OK, now we have a freighter to find. A whole ship is in the wind."

* * * *

The interview of Marko Brunelli that afternoon was short and not all that sweet. It was more of a shot across the bow and both parties knew that was what it was. It was conducted at police headquarters, with Burton Kahn doing the brief questioning and Brunelli's lawyer sitting at Brunelli's shoulder and perpetually whispering in his ear. The mobster was cool enough, though, that the presence of his lawyer hardly seemed necessary. Hodgkins was there too, sitting next to Kahn. Clint, who was watching through the one-way mirror kept his eyes pinned on the assistant D.A. most of the short time the interview lasted, looking for any sign that might appear that Hodgkins was linked to Brunelli. But the assistant D.A. was showing his cool as well.

The interview was at the police station rather than in Brunelli's office or home precisely because this was just a shot across his bow. And he obviously understood it as such, but when it was evident that serial killings at and near the docks were a target of the questioning and not just the death of the court case witness, Will Trent, Clint thought that either Brunelli's reaction of surprise was genuine or that he was a consummate actor. Clint had turned to Danny, standing next to him behind the glass, to make this observation and Danny had just grunted. Danny was very interested in pinning all of this on Brunelli.

"Why, yes," Brunelli answered, "I do own the Christopher Hotel. A recent acquisition; I'm still in the process of renovating it."

"Yes, I am quite distressed that a man was found murdered there this morning. But it's the docks area. Not the best part of town—yet. I'm trying to help clean it up—the whole area. It's certainly not good for my business to have people murdered there."

"Yes, I was there yesterday, as a matter of fact. As I said, I'm renovating the hotel. I have to show up there frequently for surprise inspections. You know how the trades are in this city. You have to ride their butts to keep them working."

"No, I'm sorry, I can't help you there. I didn't see the young man in the hotel yesterday. No, I didn't get down to Chris's bar in the basement during my inspection yesterday."

"Me? Last night. Ah, yes, I was with a young man. He's a great bartender and I was trying to convince him to move over to Chris's bar. I'm trying to upgrade that club. Yes, I can give you his name. Yes. His name is Greg Garrison. He works at The Dugout club now. I'm sure you can find him there almost any time—at least until I can convince him to come work at Chris's."

"So sorry I couldn't help more. But, you know, you could have asked me these questions at my office. I didn't need to be brought down here. I think my lawyer will be talking to someone in the mayor's office about the police wasting their time—and mine—like this."

Clint almost shrank back from the window, because Brunelli was now staring directly at him—just as if he could see through the glass.

The interview with Greg Garrison, conducted by Danny, with Clint once again behind the glass with Burton Kahn and Neil Paxton, didn't go any better. Garrison was nervous without appearing to be surprised about what he was being asked about, and it was evident that Brunelli's people had gotten to him and coached him before he was brought in. Still, what he said was telling.

"Did he say I was with him last night?"

"Yes, Greg, Marko Brunelli said you were with him most of the night—at his home on Long Island. That isn't true?"

"Yes, of course, it's true," the blond bartender said, obviously flustered. "He brought me in because he wants me to come work for him at Chris's. I'm a bartender, and he's jazzing up things at the Christopher Hotel. Making changes."

"He had you brought to his house to offer you a job?" Danny knew how to put just enough disbelief in his voice to keep a suspect off guard.

"Yes."

"And it took him all night to offer you the job?"

"Hey, man. Do we really have to get into that stuff? It's private. I was with him most of the night. I know he didn't go anywhere. What else do you need to know? This doesn't have to get around, does it?"

"Most of the night? Until when exactly?"

"Damn. I went to sleep, OK? He was there when I went to sleep and he was there when I woke up."

"And all that time he was offering you a job, right?"

"Fuck you," Garrison said, not being able to hold it back. Danny could have gotten all in his face at that point, but he liked how Garrison was answering—and how it would likely come across in a courtroom if he answered the same way there. All the same, he couldn't resist pushing it home.

"You can't just say the guy was screwing you? You work in a gay bar and you dress like you are now and you're worried about your reputation?"

Garrison crossed his arms on his chest and withdrew into himself. Kahn rapped lightly on the window, and Danny must have gotten the point that they didn't want Garrison just shutting down on them, so he changed the tone of his voice.

"I'm just confused, Greg. You didn't seem sure when I first asked you that you were, in fact, with Marko Brunelli last night."

"I was with him, OK? And I was in his bed and we were having sex, OK? It's just that I got flustered. I've never been called in and grilled like this before. And how am I to know what Mr. Brunelli wants known about who he screws?"

"OK, you can go now, Greg, but if you think of something else you want to tell us, be sure to call. And, Greg . . . this wasn't grilling. If you hold back on us or if you don't tell us

61

the truth, you'll see what grilling is all about. And try to remember that there are prison-time sentences for perjury." Danny was using the softer voice tone, but his words quite evidently had the desired effect of making Greg Garrison scared.

"I was with him all night last night and he didn't go anywhere—except to the john a couple of times. That's what happened."

"He's lying about something," Danny said when Greg was gone and he came into the room adjacent to the interview room.

"Right," Kahn said. "And maybe a good prosecutor can make his claim that he was with Brunelli last night look as iffy as you did in there. But we'll just have to see how that works out. If he says in court what he just said, they'll have an opening to discredit his statement."

"Oh, how?" Clint asked. He knew what the other two didn't know—that Greg, in fact, was being fucked by Brunelli and that his claim he spent the night at Brunelli's Long Island house was a credible one. Clint had already been at that house when he was there and it was pretty clear that Greg was going to be spending that night in Brunelli's bed.

"He lied about never being in a police interview room before," Kahn said. "We ran a check on him before bringing him in. He's been in prison already for lying about engaging in gay activity and for forced sodomy. He was a witness in a case and while the case was going on he was charged with forced sodomy and chewed up by the prosecution in his attempt to be an alibi and character witness for a guy subsequently convicted of murder. If he tries it again with Brunelli, the prosecutors will chew him up again."

"So, I say we just leave this as is," Danny said, "and let that happen if we can find anything else that can get Brunelli into court for these murders."

"We might have something," Neil Paxton said. He had been gone for part of Garrison's interview, because he got a cell phone call and had to leave the room to take it. But he came back in when Danny did.

"What?" Kahn asked.

"I got a call from the lab. The guy who murdered the witness, Will Trent, wasn't as careful as he was when he poked and murdered the others. Pubic hairs were found in Trent's channel. The lab tests and run of the DNA through CODIS have just come back."

"And?" Danny this time.

"Two guys were on him. The tests came up positive for Brunelli, which is what we were looking for. And another guy, name of Jack Wilde, was inside him too. And he comes up positive as Brunelli's personal bodyguard."

Jocko, Clint thought. They can link Brunelli through his bodyguard, Jocko. I wonder what DNA they could pull off me from both of those bruisers, he went on to think.

"Good linking," Kahn said. "But let's not pull Brunelli and this bodyguard back in just now. Now that we have a link, it's time to talk to the D.A. and start putting the screws to Brunelli in our research."

"To the D.A. directly? Not through Hodgkins?" It was Paxton who asked the question, but it was Clint who Kahn turned toward to give an answer.

"I think to the D.A. directly. I think we'll keep this close to our vests for the moment. This is a case we want to stick on Brunelli if we can get him to court on it. He's been entirely too slippery in his previous brushes with the court system."

"We may only need enough to get him in a cell at Riker's Island without bail," Danny said.

Everyone turned their questioning eyes in his direction.

"Well, he's got so many enemies in the underworld that we may only need to get him away from his minders and trapped in a cell he can't slither out of, and then someone might save us money and court time."

When the stares continued, Danny said. "What? We all know he's guilty of enough to fry—beyond these cases. I, for one, ain't gonna cry crocodile tears if someone else takes care of him for us."

* * * *

Clint didn't know if he would have done anything differently when he walked up the stairs to his apartment that evening if he'd been paying better attention. Chances are it wouldn't have mattered a bit. When he opened the door to the apartment, noticing that he didn't have to turn over as many locks as he usually set and had entered his living room, he just shrugged and moved to the kitchen area. He had to admit he wasn't thinking too hard about his routine when he'd last left the apartment . . . but . . . it *was* a routine, and he was thinking clearer now. While he was taking his suit jacket off and draping it over the back of a chair pulled into the kitchen island and facing the living area, he was slipping his cell phone out of his trousers pocket, stroking the buttons that would hook him up with Danny, and dropping the phone in his jacket pocket.

Then and only then did he lift his head to look into the eyes of Jocko, who was sitting in an armchair at the other end of the living area.

His mind was racing. How had they traced where he lived? Was it that the black guy who had brought him home from the cemetery had been sent by Brunelli? Had they known all along where he lived? And he'd told that guy he was a homicide cop. Had Brunelli known that all along as well? What a chump he'd been. Danny had told him to keep in touch at all times and he'd brushed him off tonight. Clint had told him he just wanted to come home and have one night at home not thinking about anything. He'd promised he wouldn't go out the bars. And he had fully intended not to. And so, here he was, alone and without backup.

"Hello Jocko," he said. Hoping that somehow what he was saying was going out on the telephone.

"You walked out on the boss yesterday. That wasn't a real bright thing to do."

"He actually walked out on me Jocko. He didn't tell me to stay. And he left. For all I knew he'd be bringing someone else back to the hotel room. And then there I'd be. That would be an awkward moment. He's always been able to find me. I waited around for a long time before I left. And speaking of finding me, how did you find where I lived?"

"I followed you that night the boss had me drive you back. I knew you didn't live where I left you off. I parked and followed you here."

Clint tried not to show his relief. Maybe they didn't know he was a cop after all. "OK, so you found me here. You can go back and tell the boss that you found me—coming home to my apartment alone. And that I didn't mean any disrespect when I left the Christopher the other night. I didn't know he'd want me to stay."

"He wants me to bring you back."

"Tonight? To the Christopher or to his house out on Long Island?" Clint was saying this with the hope that either Danny or his voicemail could hear it.

"It will be a long drive—in case you want to take a piss or something before we go."

"Ah, out to Long Island then. No, I'm good. We can go." Clint started around the kitchen island in the direction of the door to the outer corridor.

"Don't you want to take your coat?"

"Nah, it's OK. It would be just one more thing to have to take off."

Although he showed a bit of irritation that Clint hadn't been in the Christopher Hotel bedroom when he'd returned the previous day, Brunelli didn't show any signs when Clint was delivered to his Long Island estate basement playroom of having been leaned on by the police earlier that day or that he had anything to worry about concerning whatever they were investigating. Must have balls of steel, Clint thought as he was being strapped up, face down, on a padded-top restraint board.

He'd seen the apparatus the first time he'd been in the basement playroom and it had set his juices going. He had been restrained and fucked on one before, but nothing this elaborate. It was a platform, with a padded vinyl top and wide enough so that his arms were stretched out straight from his sides and cuffed flat at the wrists on the table top. A more heavily padded wedge under his belly lifted his torso up and back, putting his butt up in the air and his knees in a wide-stanced kneeling position, with his ankles cuffed to the surface of the platform. His cock and balls went through an opening in the rear side of the wedge and a mesh cage trapped and separated the ball sack. His head was in a harness at the top edge of the table with his chin in a cup at the table's edge.

Clint was completely incapacitated on the platform by Jocko and one of the guards who had been patrolling the rim of the sunken patio leading to the basement room before Brunelli appeared in a robe, which he shucked off, revealing his massive, hairy, powerful body, already in half erection.

"Comfortable?"

"For now," Clint answered through clinched teeth.

"You aren't afraid?"

"Yes. But excited too. Don't make me wait."

"Ah, you've done this before. You never cease to amaze me, Mr. Movie Star. I still want you working for me—working under me. I want you here all of the time. I don't want to have to send Jocko out to fetch you. I want you here for when I feel the urge for you. We got a room upstairs just for you. All ready."

Clint didn't respond. He was still unsure of going this far into the investigation—certainly not without the squad being more in on it. Jocko's appearance in his apartment had unnerved him—that he could be touched that easily without any backup in place. He hoped that Danny had heard whatever went out on that cell phone. If he said "yes" to working under Brunelli and living here right now, would he ever get out of this house again? Would Danny and the rest of the squad have any idea this was where he was?

Brunelli was walking circles around the platform. He had a switch in his hand with leather prongs and was lightly swishing it on Clint's exposed buttocks, thighs, and back. Clint grunted for him and pulled at the restraints, to no avail.

"Ah, I see that you are getting a little nervous now," Brunelli said. "I can see the glistening of sweat now." The switch stung against Clint's buttocks a little more forcefully, and he gave a gasp followed by a little moan.

"Please," he murmured.

"Please what, Mr. Movie Star."

"Please don't make me wait for it. Fuck me please. Ride me." Clint wanted to get on with it.

"This session isn't just about pleasure, I'm afraid," Brunelli said, his voice taking a harder edge. "You were found cruising the bars, picking up who knows what, and you left the hotel the other

66

day. Jocko had to come get you today. A little lesson is needed on who is the boss here."

Brunelli lashed out with the hand whip, striking Clint five times on the buttocks, back, and thighs.

Clint howled and strained ineffectively against the restraints.

"I'll bet you liked that," Brunelli said, his voice a little breathless from the exertion. "You're such a slut. Jocko, go under and check how much our guest liked that."

"Hard as a rock," a muffled voice reported from under the platform. Clint felt the hand on his cock under the platform.

"Oh god, now, please!" he cried out. He was only half acting.

"Shit. I'm too fuckin' hard already too," Brunelli said. He mounted the platform and then Clint's ass and began pumping him hard. Clint sighed a satisfied sigh. He not only had shortened the punishment but now he also had a thick cock working inside him.

Brunelli went on for a while, with grunts and groans and passing on instructions to Jocko and the other guard.

While Clint was being fucked by the mobster, the other two were busy adding toys. Weights were applied to extend Clint's balls down toward the floor, and a mouth attachment was added to the head gear, which stretched Clint's lips wide and depressed his tongue. A mouth began working his cock from underneath and Jocko was standing at his head with his hands holding Clint's head and his cock using the open channel the mouth gear had created.

Clint came before Jocko did, and Jocko came before Brunelli did.

"There you are," Clint heard Brunelli say as he was lifting his weight off Clint's pelvis.

Clint moved his eyes to where he could get a fleeting look of Brunelli putting his robe back on and taking the arm of a blond guy and moving across to a door into the interior of the house. Greg. Greg Garrison. Clint was sure that was who it was.

At the door, Brunelli turned, and said to Jocko, "Let any of the guards use him who want to and then take him home. We'll be talking again about my offer in a day or two, Mr. Movie Star.

Remember, the rest of tonight was because you weren't where I left you when I came back."

Unless he had lost count, Clint figured he was fucked by four different guys while restrained on the platform before he was released and permitted to shower in an adjacent locker room. Then Jocko drove him home, came up to the apartment with him, and pushed him into his bedroom and onto his back on the bed after he'd stripped. Jocko tied Clint's wrists to the headboard, wishboned his legs, and took his own, leisurely—and very satisfying to Clint—turn at the fuck.

Clint had to work his own wrists free when Jocko had gone. When he'd done so—and taken a piss and a quick shower— he went straight to his suit jacket at the kitchen island and fished into his pocket. He fiddled with his cell phone but could find no evidence that his earlier message had gotten through to Danny.

He rang Danny's number. A hoarse-voiced Danny answered. Clint could hear the heavy breathing of someone else in the background.

"Clint? You OK?"

"Yes, I just wondered if anything was up?"

"You could say that. But you got a problem? Need anything?"

So, he hadn't gotten any distress message from Clint. "No, no. Everything's fine. I just thought I'd call and check in."

"You want that I come over there."

"No, it's fine. I'll see you in the morning at the precinct. Enjoy yourself."

He clicked off. This was entirely too much risk. He needed to keep Danny—and maybe the rest of the squad—closer to him. And maybe he needed to find someplace else to bunk out until this case was over.

They were determined to nail Brunelli. But the strange thing was that Brunelli wasn't acting at all like he was cornered. He was offering Clint a longer, closer arrangement, and he didn't act at all like a man under the microscope. And Clint—and it looks like the similar looking Greg—had been with Brunelli multiple times now without getting murdered. Clint—and maybe the rest of the squad—needed to rethink where they were going with this.

Chapter Six: Last Bus to Riker's

"You're there," Danny said it as if he was surprised that Clint picked up on the phone call. "You alone and home?"

"Yes, Danny, I'm on the line and home and alone. And unless I haven't opened my eyes yet, it's still dark out. What gives?" He rolled over to a sitting position in his bed and turned on the bedside lamp. It was barely 5:00 a.m.

"Got a big one this time. Not part of the serial killings, but it's at the Christopher again. Kahn is calling out all hands. Come on down. Just follow the line of cops up to the third floor."

"Not part of the serial killings? For sure?"

"Yes, for sure. It's a judge. Not blond, not all that good looking, not in his late twenties or early thirties—but died with his pants off in a gay hotel and with a dildo shoved up his ass. The mayor's office is trying to keep the lid on, but it won't be long before it's all over town, I'm sure."

"OK, OK, I'll be there as soon as I've showered and ladled in some coffee."

"You need to be sooner, I think, if I've read Kahn's summons correctly. For the good of all of us, take the shower and forget the coffee."

"Fuck you very much. You don't want me any sooner than those two things happen. Trust me on that. But I'll be there pronto."

Clint padded into the kitchen and got the coffee pot going. Then it was straight to the toilet and the shower. His decision to go with the five-o'clock-shadow look would pay dividends today. He was showered, toweled off, his teeth brushed, dressed, and a cup of coffee gulped down in one long, well-practiced, fluid motion, and then he was in his Camaro gliding through the only-now-awakening streets to the lower Manhattan docks area.

A judge. Must be more than just any old judge for the police to be revved up this fast.

Danny had been right; he had no trouble finding the room he was looking for at the Christopher. Cops were lined up three deep inside the building, trying to look concerned, but looking more amused. Outside of the building, though, you couldn't have told what was happening. All of the cop cars must be parked on other streets, he thought, as he came in. You wouldn't know anything was happening inside the hotel. He decided that this was the way the mayor's office wanted it, so this was the way the police were playing it. Most of the cops must have been pulled out of bed and had come down in their own cars, like he did, anyway.

He got looks all the way up the stairs. The beat cops knew about the Special Homicide Unit mostly in rumor, but most of them knew it to the extent that they recognized the detectives of the squad. Although most of the cops posted up the stairs knew little about the man found dead in the hotel room overhead, they knew he was important enough to pull the police out in force. And they knew what sort of hotel this was and that guys from the Special Homicide Unit were coming in by the ones and twos.

If they hadn't known what type of hotel the Christopher was before, they certainly knew it now—from the type of patrons who had been pulled out of their rooms and gathered in the lounge off the front lobby. The male rent boys congregated to one side, looking slightly irritated at the interruption of their work—well, mostly of their income stream. In the chairs and couches in the center of the room, however, were their johns—in various stages of undress—but all uniformly looking dejected, embarrassed, and worried. Most of them were doing their best to disappear into the wallpaper, but that just wasn't working in the glare of the hotel lobby lights. These men ranged in age from their twenties to their sixties and most looked like they were slumming over from Wall Street. The guys in their twenties and thirties who had nothing to hide in their sexuality were scattered around the periphery of the room, paired up as they had been when they came into the hotel, and looking either bored or curious about what had rousted them out of a night of pleasure.

Clint took the stairs two by two and moved swiftly down the third-floor corridor to one of the hotel rooms that must have been recently refurbished in Brunelli's renovation of the place. Danny, Neil Paxton, Burton Kahn, and a couple of other guys from the squad were gathered near the door, giving room for the forensic folks to do their preliminary work.

The body was still spread-eagled on the bed, on its back, its slightly flabby arms raised toward the headboard where the wrists were cuffed. The cock was flaccid but was sheathed by a condom. As Danny had said, the pistol handle of a black, rubber dildo was sticking out of the judge's ass. It was evident from what could be seen inside the condom that the man had had an ejaculation before dying. There was a plastic bag over his head, plastered to his face, a rather obvious indication that he'd died of asphyxiation. The dead man was a bit chunky and well-pelted, but not in all that bad a condition—other than being dead—for a man who must have been in his late forties or early fifties. No, this didn't look like it was connected to their current case at all—other than the Christopher being the same place the last victim had been found. But the last victim hadn't gotten this level of attention from the police in the aftermath.

Even with the plastic plastered to his face, the man looked familiar to Clint, and Clint wondered if he was someone he knew well from some court case he'd testified in.

"It's Judge Pendleton. Charles Pendleton, of the city court," Kahn said.

"Don't know the name. Think I sort of recognize the face—what I can see of it," Clint answered.

"You just saw him the other day," Danny said. "He's the judge in the current Brunelli trial. First the witness gone and then, when the judge wouldn't stop the case, he gets wiped out. And this is Brunelli's hotel. A few too many coincidences."

"Yeah, a lot of coincidences. And more than a few too many. Like anyone with brains would murder a judge in his trial in his own hotel," Clint said, mostly under his breath, but he knew that Danny heard him.

"Enough to bring Brunelli in again, don't you think, Lieutenant?" Danny continued, talking directly to Kahn and ignoring a scowling Clint. "Enough maybe, after grilling him, to make an arrest and get him processed and away from his bodyguards."

"You don't need much evidence, do you, Danny?" Clint asked. He was already running the previous evening through his mind. He'd been with Brunelli himself—and then the blond bartender, Greg, had been brought in. How much of the night did that engage Brunelli?

"Got that right," Danny said. "Best kind of justice for a guy like that. He's making a joke of the courts. So we let him be got in a more direct way. Save the courts time and money—and," he gestured to the bed as he said it, "bent judges."

Clint turned to Kahn, resisting the urge to snap back that the judge wasn't any more bent in that direction than Danny or he himself were. "Any idea on a time of death?"

"He's still warm, the medical examiner says," Kahn answered. "Must not have been more than a couple of hours."

"And we're right here, not long after it happened?"

"Got a call—an anonymous call that we'd find someone important here. Gave the room number and all."

"Ah, an anonymous call," Clint said. The expression he flashed for both Kahn and Danny showed what he thought about that call.

"So, can we go get him and bring him in for questioning?" Danny asked, ignoring Clint's expression of disbelief.

"Yes," Kahn answered. "The mayor's office wants to pull out all stops. This is Brunelli's hotel, and he's the target of a case the judge was trying. Nothing about this looks like a simple gay assignation gone bad. The medical examiner found a needle mark and will test for a drug that might have been given him to knock him out—although the way he's tied up, the plastic bag could have gone over his head without that. Other trace material was found on him too. We don't want anyone rushing to judgment on what the judge actually was involved in. With the mayor's offices' backing we've put a priority on the testing of that. I wouldn't be surprised if they find that trace going back to Brunelli and maybe his bodyguard as well, as with the Will Trent case—and maybe we can get that while we still have Brunelli in interrogation."

"That wouldn't surprise me a bit either," Danny said, his voice full of hope.

"It wouldn't surprise me either," Clint muttered, somewhat more sardonically.

"So, you wanna go help me with the arrest?" Danny said to Clint when they pulled out into the hallway to give more room for the gurney to get in to move the body. "It might rattle his cage more to see you as a cop. It might get him to say things he wouldn't otherwise."

"Maybe at the precinct," Clint answered. "I'd like to go over the reports on the court case files—including the ones on that guy who alibied Brunelli earlier—that Greg Garrison guy. Are those on your desk?"

"Yeah."

"Well, when I first come face to face with Brunelli, I think I should have a very good grasp of the whole background, don't you? I think that would unnerve him the most."

"Yeah, maybe you're right. See you at headquarters, with our bird in a cage. And who knows what might happen while he's caged?"

"I'd be a lot happier if you didn't keep saying things like that, Danny. That's too much taking judgment in our own hands, and that's not our job."

Clint stood and watched Danny leave. He didn't know who was closer to this, Danny or him, but, although he wanted to see justice done, he didn't want it to be a stolen justice. And it seemed to Clint that this was what Danny wanted now. He wanted to get Brunelli any way he could. But if Brunelli hadn't done this—if someone else had done it—where would the justice for them come from? And where was the satisfaction if Brunelli wasn't being punished for something he actually did? If Brunelli wasn't behind the serial killings, wouldn't they just keep on happening?

* * * *

The paperwork piled in front of Clint was confusing. It wasn't just because there was a lot of it but also because, as he read through it, he could see patterns emerging. Unfortunately, he could see more than one pattern emerging, each almost, but not quite, holding together as a pattern. And each not that much better as a definitive explanation than the next one. It was enough, however, that he wanted to slow today down—for them all to just pull back in the squad room and talk it all out. But if they did that, and all of the relevant information came out, which he felt would need to, he would be admitting to multiple infractions of their code. Not only did he have a relationship with their target, but, more important, he had kept it and other facts in this investigation to himself. He didn't even have Danny to fall back on for support. He'd kept some of it from Danny too. No one would be more angry and hurt by what Clint hadn't said than his partner would be. He'd seen this happen between partners before, and it had put them dangerously off balance. Nothing could be the same again between them, or between Clint and the rest of the squad. Nobody could fully trust anyone else to have their back anymore, and if your partner didn't have your back out on the street, you were as good as dead.

He felt it was something he had to do soon, though. The pattern here was so much more complex than they were permitting for in their rush to get Brunelli nailed.

He was about to rise and go to Burton Kahn's office when Danny entered from the corridor and, with a triumphant expression marching across his face, announced that Brunelli and his lawyer were down in the tombs, in Interview Room B.

"And the bodyguard, Jack Wilde?" Kahn asked when he came out of his office.

"Haven't nabbed him yet, but we have a search out for him," Danny said.

Paxton came in at that point and said, "A couple of the detectives have gone to pick Greg Garrison up. When we took Brunelli, he was saying he was with Garrison last night. He didn't even wait for us to ask—or to tell him more than that we were arresting him for the murder of Judge Pendleton—before he was claiming an alibi."

"OK, Neil and I will take Brunelli," Kahn said. "Danny, you and Clint can take Garrison when he comes in. You know what to ask—and what not to lead him with."

"What about the assistant D.A.?" Paxton asked. "He wants to be in on all of this. Is he on his way?"

"Couldn't get hold of him," Kahn answered. "His office doesn't know where he is. He hasn't come in yet today and should have. Anyway, I'm just as glad he's not going to be in on this interview—and don't ask me why."

Ah ha, Clint thought as he contemplated the absence of Hodgkins. A thread for that pattern maybe.

They started out by all gathering around the one-way mirror looking into Interview Room B. Kahn liked to build in these moments where just the suspect and his or her attorney were in the room alone, because what they had to say—or not to say—to each other without the cops present often was the most revealing testimony to come out of the interview. The lawyers knew it wasn't a safe place to talk, of course, but their clients often felt so bottled up and ready to explode that the lawyer couldn't contain them.

It was clear that Brunelli was unhinged—more so than Clint had ever observed before. And he was after his attorney with the repeated question, "Where is he? He should be here. I need out of here. Now. I can't go to prison. Even for an hour."

The attorney kept trying to shush him, obviously knowing they were being watched, and he eventually pulled Brunelli's ear to his mouth. What he told Brunelli made the mobster look straight at the one-way mirror and then subside in a deflated, "not-used-to-being-powerless" state. He turned his head from the wall with the one-way window, but as there was a mirror on the other wall too and cameras beyond that to provide video to the "watch" room, his frustrated, helpless expression wasn't lost on the detectives.

That didn't stop him from murmuring, "Not even for an hour. Can't be locked up for even a minute."

"He wondering where his bodyguard is?" It was Danny who asked.

"Maybe," Kahn answered. But he was looking at Clint, who was looking back at him. Their shared guess was that Brunelli had expected Assistant D.A. Henry Hodgkins to sweep in and somehow get him out of this mess.

The interrogation didn't go well with Brunelli. The mobster clammed right up and wouldn't even acknowledge who he was. He was trembling enough to please all of the cops watching, though, and to keep a big frown on his lawyer's face.

When Greg Garrison was brought in to the station, Danny and Clint agreed that Danny would take him alone—that it would be best for Clint to remain something other than a cop on the case toward all parties in the investigation for now. And Danny was delighted with what Garrison told him.

"Last night? I was tending bar until about 8:00 and then I took in a movie—sure, I have the ticket stub somewhere if you want to see it—and then I just went back to my place and sacked out. Busy day."

"He said what? Brunelli said I was with him last night. What is this about? A judged murdered?"

Garrison paled at that point and said, "No, I wasn't with Brunelli last night." And then when pressed, with two murders and a possible charge of being an accessory to murder dangling before his eyes, he owned up to not having been with Brunelli on any of the dates he'd said he was.

He was very convincing, but he made Clint's brow knit. Clint knew Garrison had been around Brunelli a couple of those evenings, including the previous night. Yet another thread for the competing patterns Clint was seeing. They all needed to fit together somehow. This was the one that made the least sense to Clint—at least for now.

Clint left the interrogation and went back to the reports on his desk that he had been reading through. There would be video of the questioning, and he could take his mind off the reports he had been reading. That's where Danny found him when he returned to the squad room from the tombs. The triumphant look Clint saw in his partner's eyes was explanation enough of how the interview with Brunelli had gone.

"He's on his way to Riker's now," Danny said as he sat down at this desk.

"Just like that?" Clint asked.

"The results on the DNA trace on the judge's body came in while Brunelli was still here. It was all the D.A. needed. Both Brunelli and his bodyguard were with the judge before he died."

"Because their DNA was found on his body? You don't find that a bit strange? That a mobster would kill a judge in his own hotel and leave his trace on him?" Clint was trying to keep his cool.

"That's what arrogance gets you. Now the countdown starts. We should do a pool among the guys on how long Brunelli lasts at Riker's. You should of seen him. I thought he was going to shit his pants when we arrested him and told him where he was going to be processed and held."

"Did he confess?" Clint asked.

"Of course not. His kind never do. He probably thinks he can wriggle out of it. His lawyer was looking a little sick too, though."

"How closely did you check out these background reports on Greg Garrison?" Clint asked, holding up some of the paper he'd taken from Danny's desk.

"I know they paint him as an unreliable witness," Danny answered, "but we're getting much more evidence than that on Garrison. And it was Brunelli who said he was with Garrison on the occasions of the murders."

"Did you see what happened to Garrison in that trail he was a witness in? That he was thrown out as a character witness because he was put on trial himself for forceful sodomy?"

"Yeah, I saw that. So?"

"Did you see that the prosecuting attorney in both Garrison's case and that of his friend was Charles Pendleton, who wasn't a judge yet?"

"No. I didn't see that." Danny was beginning to be exasperated. "What are you trying to do here, Clint? We got the guy. It isn't complicated."

"And did you read his testimony?" Clint continued as if Danny hadn't interrupted, "that he not only thought his friend was innocent of that murder, but that both he and his friend said that it was a mob hit—by Brunelli's people? And did you see that Garrison was convicted of his crime but was released early—with Charles Pendleton, now a judge, signing the release order?"

77

"Where is this coming from, Clint? And where are you going with it?"

"It's both coming from and going to everything here being just a little too conveniently pointing to Brunelli and Garrison's involvement with both Brunelli and Pendleton being just a bit too coincidental."

Danny stared at Clint with a face full of stubborn resistance.

"Greg Garrison lied to you about not being with Brunelli last evening, Danny. Brunelli or his bodyguard—or both of them—could have killed Pendleton this morning, but Garrison lied about not being with him last night."

"And how do you know this?"

Clint didn't answer. He just sat there and looked intently at Danny.

"It's because you were there last night too, isn't it?" Danny suddenly was close to exploding. This was what Clint was afraid of; this is why he had spiraled down so much into being too closely involved in this investigation—having to hack it alone, because he knew the reaction Danny would have to anything he did with Brunelli. And, damn it, he didn't even know the guy was Brunelli when it had gotten started.

"Garrison was at Brunelli's house on Long Island last night, Danny. Now just calm down. It isn't just that's he's lying about that. Why is he with Brunelli at all, given this old court case of his? And what's this about a Pendleton angle? There's just too much overlapping here, Danny."

"You continued to see Brunelli? And let him fuck you as recently as last night?" Danny couldn't get off that subject.

And then they both were interrupted. Neil Paxton and a few of the other detectives who had been out on assignment were streaming into the room.

"Gather around, ladies," Paxton was bellowing. "Can't rest on our laurels on getting Brunelli behind bars. We have news on the serial killings case."

"I keep telling you," Danny turned from Clint and called out to Paxton. "Brunelli's good for those too. You'll see that I'm right."

"We have this other avenue we're pursuing," Paxton retorted, "and unless we can link Brunelli to the *Larnaka Star*, he might not be on this pathway."

"The *Larnaka Star*?" Danny said. "That's half way to Bermuda now. We've got several days before we pick up on that freighter."

"Not so. You weren't there when we learned from the Bermuda end that the freighter wasn't expected there this week. The port authority belatedly told us the freighter didn't leave for Bermuda at all. It just went up to Boston to take on some cargo. It returned this morning. These guys here served the warrant and searched the ship after the crew got off. They got the crew lists and schedules we wanted. But, more important, they found what could be the kill site."

"The kill site?" Clint asked.

"Yes," Paxton said. "There's a locker down in the bowels of the freighter with a cot and cuff attachments. And some blood. We took samples, but then we got out of there. It's up to Kahn to decide where we take it from here."

As if on cue, Burton Kahn was coming out of his office. He had a serious, concerned expression on his face.

"They got him," Kahn said in a subdued voice. "He didn't even have time to get processed and to his cell. When the bus pulled into receiving at Riker's, he was already dead on the bus. Knifed."

"Brunelli?" Paxton asked.

"Yes," Kahn answered.

Clint looked into Danny's face. The look of supreme satisfaction in his face made Clint want to puke. "Just tell me that this wasn't your doing, Danny—that you didn't arrange it."

"No. I didn't have to," Danny said. "Didn't I tell you that all that needed to be done was to get him away from his people."

"I heard that," Kahn said. "And I don't want to hear any more of it. And I don't want to hear it coming back from the outside, either. What is done is done. We're not going to stop following leads on the docks serial killing investigation, either. We don't want to spook the killer, if it's someone on the freighter crew—and if it wasn't Brunelli. I don't think for a minute that it was, though. So, we'll leave the locker you found unprocessed for now. I trust you have the ship's captain buttoned down, Neil?"

"Yep. He's not going to talk to any of the crew about this."

"OK, so, divvy up the crew member names among teams and tomorrow we'll round them up and start working on them." Kahn turned to go back to his office.

"What about the Wilde guy, Brunelli's bodyguard?" Paxton asked. "Brunelli's history, but Wilde is in the wind, and his trace was on the bodies of the judge and the witness as well."

"Oh, I forgot. The call on Brunelli knocked that out of my mind," Kahn answered. "I got that call just before I got the call on Brunelli. They picked up Wilde—down in Maryland, on I-95. And, surprise, surprise, they picked up Assistant D.A. Hodgkins with him."

When he said this, Kahn was giving Clint a look.

"What's that all about?" Danny asked.

"We'll have to see," Kahn answered. "Wheels within wheels. I wouldn't be surprised to know that Brunelli had Hodgkins in his pocket. I've seen some evidence of that. But putting the two together that we picked up may mean this was all a power play to get Brunelli out of the way."

Wheels within wheels was certainly what Clint was thinking too, as he reached for his share of the sailor files Paxton was handing out.

When everyone was settling down, he looked over at Danny, who wasn't as euphoric as he had been when he heard that Brunelli was dead. Clint was afraid he was brooding again about Clint not having stopped seeing Brunelli. Not that he had had a choice, Clint thought. Brunelli had always just taken what he wanted. Somehow Clint had to make Danny understand that. It just happened the first time, when Brunelli was just a thuggish-looking guy. Clint knew that wouldn't fly with Danny though. He'd counter with "a thug with a bodyguard, so guaranteed bad news."

What, Clint wondered, would have happened if he'd told Brunelli right off the top that he was a cop? It could have gone several ways then, and not too many of them good for Clint. But he knew he was kidding himself. He, Clint, wouldn't have called it off. He wanted what Brunelli had had to give.

"Danny," Clint said in a low voice.

No response.

"I was thinking that I might come back to your place with you for tonight."

"I don't think that would be wise," Danny said in a voice that was half choke and half growl. "I know you like it rough, but I don't think I could control my temper with you tonight."

There was no more conversation between the two. And in the silence Clint's mind raced on all that was happening in these investigations and on that phrase: wheels within wheels. This wasn't even close to being over where he was concerned.

Chapter Seven: Greg's Story

There had to be a way of opening this guy up, Clint thought as he walked into The Dugout bar the next afternoon. I've got to find it; I can't just let this ride like Danny wants me to. I hope he hasn't disappeared on us.

Greg Garrison hadn't disappeared. He was working the bar at The Dugout and looking just as happy as he could be.

He must know, Clint thought as he bellied up to the bar near where Greg, one of three guys working behind the bar, was dispensing drinks and ordered a beer.

"Hi," he said to Greg as the man tapped his beer. He used a friendly smile on the bartender. Clint didn't know at this point whether Greg would recognize him or not.

"Hi yourself," Greg answered. The greeting had made him look up into Clint's face. "I know you, don't I? You been in here before?"

"Just the once. But there was some excitement we both were involved in that night. I think we have a mutual acquaintance—or had."

Greg's eyes narrowed, and then he realized where he'd seen Clint before—at Brunelli's house out on Long Island. A couple of times. And before that. The night Brunelli had worked him over in the back room here and told him he was on the hook for more. When he'd come back behind the bar, Brunelli had left with this guy.

Greg's eyes narrowed and his hands went to the shelf below the bar. Clint had little doubt that there was some sort of protection for the barmen lurking down there.

"I'm not here to make trouble," Clint quickly said, and then, "So you've heard? You know he's gone?"

"Yeah, I heard," Greg answered guardedly.

"You regret it? I don't."

The bartender visibly relaxed. "Yeah, I figure the world's better without him."

"Maybe we should talk," Clint said. "Can you pull away from the bar for a few?"

"Yeah, I guess so," Greg answered. He signaled to the other two bartenders that he was taking a break, tapped a beer for himself, and let Clint lead him with the palm of his hand on the small of his back over to a table in the far corner of the room.

"I don't know about you, but I was hoping someone else wouldn't get to him first," Clint said when they were seated and had their heads close together across the table.

"You weren't into him?"

"Some of it was over the top, even for me. The fucking was OK, but, no. He came for me—or sent his goon after me. I don't usually bottom. I like it the other way. But I didn't mind him doing me, because I had a grudge and was working out how I could get him back on that. I bet he just grabbed you too and rough sexed you too, didn't he?"

"Yes. He was an animal."

"The one time I was in here I saw you coming out of the back in a daze with him following you. I can see why he wanted you; you looked good to me too. Was that your first time with him and did he give you a choice?"

Clint was gradually working on the guy's vanity and suggesting possibilities. He wanted to get his defenses down, and Clint would try anything to get Greg talking. If it took fucking him to get him to open up, that's what Clint would do. He could tell by the looks Greg game him that the guy was interested.

"No, he didn't give me a choice," Greg answered with the anger in his voice that Clint was cultivating. "He as much beat me up as fucked me. And he told me it was just a start."

"And then he kept sending for you, didn't he?"

"Yes."

"Same with me. You deserve better than that, a good-looking guy like you. You should get it slow and easy, with a lot of loving. I could do that for you." Clint had worked Greg's polo shirt up from the front and had palmed the man's belly. Greg was panting. He put a hand on Clint's forearm, and Clint knew it wasn't a gesture to try to make him remove the hand. Clint had already seen at Brunelli's the effect of someone putting their hand on Greg's belly.

"You say you top guys?" Greg asked in a dreamy whisper. "The only times I've seen you—"

"I can go both ways. I prefer top, especially when I see a guy as enticing as you. Every time I saw you with Brunelli, I was thinking about it being me—of Brunelli being me, and also thinking that I'd be better to you than that fuckin' mobster was. If the guy is right, I can really enjoy topping him. And he can really enjoy it too. You think you might be the right guy for me?"

That much was true—Clint did take on the top role when he needed to. And he did think Greg deserved better than Brunelli.

They fucked on a small bed in one of the rooms for that purpose at the rear of the building. Clint spooned Greg into his belly and wrapped an arm around the other man's neck, bringing their faces together in deep kisses while Clint side split Greg from behind. Greg was putty in his hands, purring and moaning at the slow, deep fuck Clint gave him.

Clint felt the other man completely relax in his arms after they had both ejaculated. Greg nuzzled up into Clint, giving the detective a clear signal that he'd liked what he'd gotten.

"I'm glad you couldn't stand him either. It makes me feel good that there's someone else who feels like me." Clint was whispering in Greg's ear, continuing to soften him up, working on getting Greg to share and to push away some of this fog that covered the investigation. "It's not like me to wish anyone dead, but god knows I wished that on Brunelli. For what he did. I'm just sorry that I wasn't—"

"He did something to you too? What did he do to you?"

There it was. Garrison had a grudge against Brunelli for some past issue.

"I knew about Brunelli a long time before he fucked me. I have to admit I almost threw myself in his path. I needed to get close to him—to pay him back . . . for something. I just didn't have the plan yet and hadn't worked up the courage. I only wish . . ."

"You might have got what you wished," Greg murmured—and Clint almost flinched in his relief that he was finding the key to unlock Greg. "What did he do to you to make you feel like that?"

This would be the most delicate part. It had to be convincing—but not over the top, and Clint would have to spin it on the fly. "It was my brother," Clint said. "He got in with the wrong crowd and ended up in Brunelli's mob. I doubt he ever fit in. He was much too good. And he had a conscience. I don't know where he went wrong. Must have been while he was in Afghanistan."

"He was in Afghanistan?"

"Yeah. I don't remember where, though. He never wanted to talk about it. I think it got to him."

God, Clint thought. I forgot that Greg had been in Afghanistan too. He remembered now that this had been noted in Garrison's police file. I'll have to be very careful here, he thought. But it should help in the end.

Greg just sighed and settled into Clint's chest.

"Anyway, when he came home he was a different guy. Harder. We'd always been so close, but when he came in it was like there was a shell around him—like he didn't want me to know about all of the bad things in life he'd seen. Anyway, there were problems within the mob and Brunelli accused my brother of being a police plant. Then he stopped and got all nice, nice. But a couple of weeks later, my brother's body was found in a dumpster behind a grocery store. Turns out Brunelli had had him popped off just to flush out the real police plant in his gang. That's not something I could forget. I only wish I'd gotten around to—"

"It was pretty much the same with me," Greg muttered. Clint stopped dead in his tracks on the yarn he was spinning. This was exactly what he had hoped for.

"What do you mean?" was all he said, inviting Greg to spill it all. And spill most of it, Greg did.

"It wasn't a brother with me. It was my best friend. We'd been in Afghanistan together. He'd saved my life more than once and I'd returned the favor whenever I could. He came home before me. By the time I came home, he was in Brunelli's gang. A job was done on someone from another gang. My friend knew that Brunelli did that himself—and he told me that. But Brunelli managed to frame my friend and give him up for trial. He just, like handed my friend to him on a platter and the prosecutor took him."

"So you had no cause to be Brunelli's friend either."

"Oh, it goes much further than that. I was a character witness at the trial and was going to tell them what my friend had told me about Brunelli doing the killing himself."

"And did that do any good at the trial?" Clint had read the files. He knew it hadn't gotten that far. But he needed to know what was beyond that.

"I never got to testify. I got caught—entrapped, I think it's called. I'd always been curious, but up to that time I hadn't done anything about it."

"Curious? Curious about what?"

"Going with guys. Weeks before the trial started, a guy started coming on to me. I was working in a car dealership then—in the service department. That's what I was trained for. I haven't always been a bartender. I do this because the money is better in what guys who hit on me at the bar give me when I go with them. He did a real good job on me. Got me into the sack. I thought I was a top then; later—because of what happened later—I changed."

Clint let that sit in the air. He tried hard not to move a muscle. He wanted Greg to go on; this part he could get from the files.

"Anyway, the first thing I knew he was bringing me up on charges of raping him—forced sodomy they called it. And the prosecutor in my friend's case brought all of that out in court. Any character witness testimony I could have given then wouldn't help my friend. And no one wanted to help me, either. I found myself on trail instead of testifying in my friend's trial. We both went to prison. He was murdered there not long after—and it was there that I was changed into a bottom. Not all that willingly, but I came to be conditioned to it and to accept it as what I wanted."

"So here, us. This isn't—?"

"Shush. No. This was great. It's what I've come to want."

The two nuzzled briefly. Clint got the impression from Garrison's moans and the way he was moving his body against Clint that he wanted it again. But there were things that Clint needed to know first.

"That's bad—that Brunelli set your friend up. So, you had reason to go after Brunelli."

"Yeah, him and the prosecutor too."

Now we're getting into it, Clint thought. He started to gently stroke Greg's body, being careful to stay away from his belly. He wanted Greg talking now, not panting for it.

"The prosecutor?"

"Yeah, I've always thought that my case was some sort of put-up job between Brunelli and that prosecutor. And I'm even more sure of it from what that guy eventually did. He became a judge after that and he came to me in prison. He said he could get me out. He'd get me out if I let him fuck me whenever he wanted. I wanted out. So I agreed to it."

"And then you let him fuck you? For how long."

"Until yesterday. But no more of that. I took care of it. And Brunelli too."

"You took care of it?"

"Yeah. You don't have to feel bad that Brunelli didn't get his. That your brother isn't revenged. I did to Brunelli exactly what he'd done to others—including your brother."

"Brunelli was shivved on the bus at Riker's, I've heard," Clint said. He needed more details. He had the general picture now. But he needed details if he was going to take this to Kahn.

"I didn't know he'd get his there—at least not that quickly. But I got him there. I got him sent to Riker's. And I did it the same way he took me and my friend down. And your brother too. I'm just telling you this so you'll feel better about your brother. Brunelli got his the same way your brother did. And so did that fuckin' judge."

"You set them up, like Brunelli set your friend and you and my brother up?"

"Exactly. I made it look like Brunelli had killed a witness in a trial—even planted DNA on the body so it would lead back to Brunelli. Used that on the judge too. And I gave Brunelli an alibi for a couple of murders. And then took it back. You should

87

have seen the cops when I did that. Took it hook, line, and sinker. Of course, giving him an alibi put in their minds that I had one too—and I bet they didn't even rethink that after I took his away."

"I bet not too," Clint muttered, making a note to stick that one to Danny hard.

"I made sure I was with Brunelli right before both times so he couldn't have another alibi and would grab at my getting one, but I made sure he was finished with me early enough for me to go and do what needed to be done. I shouldn't be telling you this, I know, but I just want you to know that you don't need to go through life kicking yourself that you didn't get revenge."

"I wanted Brunelli dead," Clint said. "I can understand what you did giving him grief, but he was like a greased pig in court. He always got away. I wanted him dead."

"So did I," Greg murmured. Clint's hands had become intensively intimate now, although he was keeping them away from Greg's belly. And Clint was sliding his cock inside Greg's butt cleavage, the hard underside of the staff rubbing up and down Greg's blossoming hole. He knew now that they were going to fuck again. He was thinking more about that than that he was continuing his story, about how revealing and damning it was.

"I overheard Jocko—his bodyguard—and that D.A.'s office guy talking one night, though, at Brunelli's house. They were plotting against him too. They were trying to get him to Riker's prison. They had someone to take care of him even before he got there. I heard them because they were both pretty steamed and loud. Brunelli didn't hear them because he was in the shower after fucking me. They had expected Brunelli's bail would be rejected when the witness in the trial turned up dead. But they didn't know what I knew—that the judge was connected with Brunelli. That's how Brunelli latched on to me. The judge told him he was laying me, that he thought Brunelli would like me—he likes pretty-boy blonds with some mileage on them; but I guess you know that yourself—and that he'd be happy to share. Brunelli laughed about how the judge had gifted me to him when he told me—like I was some sort of slave, just an object. He told me that the favor he'd done for the judge to get me wasn't worth squat— how cheap I'd been. I could have killed him there and then.

"Jocko and the government lawyer wanted to take over Brunelli's operation, but they didn't want it to look like they got him killed. Some guys in his mob would still be loyal to him. So, that told me that all I needed to do was frame him up enough to get him sent to Riker's."

"And that's how it worked out," Clint said. His mind was spinning. So the bodyguard and Hodgkins were up to their necks in it too. "Yeah, thanks. That's sweet revenge."

"I got it for both of us—and maybe for others too. You just gotta keep it under your hat."

In answer, Clint put his lips to the base of Greg's neck, put his hand on Greg's belly, and pulled the man's buttocks back onto his cock. He figured—rightly apparently—that Greg would take this as agreement to his plea for silence. He also thought that if he fucked Greg to heaven now, Greg might forget that he'd told Clint much of anything. He had been panting and mewing so hard during the last part of his confession that he probably didn't even realize he was speaking.

The hand on the belly had Garrison gasping and begging for the fuck. One long, deep slide up into a channel that had already been reamed to fit Clint followed immediately by hard pumping took all further conversation away.

When they came back out into the barroom, the crowd had thickened. Greg went back behind the bar and Clint let his eyes scan the room before he left. He didn't want to make it seem like he was rushing out, but he, in fact, felt very much like rushing out and to the precinct so that he could write this up and get his notes to Kahn. And he wanted to do it before he saw Danny. Danny would just try to convince him to leave this be—that justice had been done. But it was a judgment that had been stolen. Clint didn't care that Brunelli was gone, but he felt cheated at the way that justice was stolen by Greg.

As his eyes scanned the room, they were arrested at the sight of the Russian sailor who had taken him at Chris's days before and gotten beaten by Brunelli's bodyguard. Clint almost felt like he owed the guy. There also was the point that the Russian had had a very talented cock. The Russian had also seen him and was rising. Clint could see that the Russian's friends were at the table too. The look on the Baltic hulk's face told Clint that if the Russian didn't get to Clint, that guy sure would like to.

Not now, not this evening, Clint told himself. You need to get this written up and into Kahn's hands before anyone can convince you to change your mind.

Clint saluted the Russian and his friends, but he shrugged, indicating that he really didn't have the time now. Without letting the Russian get to him to change his mind on that, he turned and walked out of the bar and straight to the subway stop. Maybe after this all spun out he could meet up with the Russian again. Clint didn't think that good fucking he had been getting when Jocko intervened was any more completed than the Russian probably did. It wasn't at all that Clint was being a tease with him.

* * * *

Clint had taken his time getting to the precinct. He'd gotten off the subway at Central Park and just walked for a couple of hours. It wasn't just Danny he had to struggle with on just letting this be. It was himself too. Greg wasn't a bad guy. He'd had his reasons. And the legal system hadn't caught up with Brunelli. It hadn't caught up with Judge Pendleton either—and probably never would have. How long had he blackmailed Greg into having sex with him now, Clint thought. Five, six years—and that after letting Greg rot in prison for a couple of years on something Pendleton had set up.

The record had shown that the guy Greg had been convicted of raping had been murdered a couple of months after that trial. And that case was still open. Greg had been in prison by then, but suggestions had been put in the record that he had something to do with that. The judge had put him in a corner. No, a cage. Greg couldn't even have gotten a job if the judge hadn't set him up in one when Greg got out of prison. And the judge had callously given Greg to Brunelli, who the judge no doubt knew was a brutal cocker.

No, Judge Pendleton deserved it. But he deserved to be caught at what he did and punished by society, not punished by a vigilante like Greg. Even the witness in Brunelli's current trial had been a thug and an uncaught murderer in his own trial. Maybe

Danny was right. Just let them go any way someone can manage to get rid of them.

Clint had been sitting on a park bench. Even when he rose to leave, he didn't know whether he was going to the precinct to write out a report on what Greg had said or go back to his apartment and forget all about what he had said. Even if he gave an accounting to Kahn, there's no saying what the police department would do with it. Garrison could just deny that he'd said any of that—and the department might welcome him doing that.

Clint found the squad room deserted when he got to the precinct. He sat down at the computer at his desk and started tapping away—with one finger of each hand. He had been scheduled for a touch typing class so many times he'd lost count. And each time a murder investigation had intervened.

He had almost finished writing up his unusual interview with Greg Garrison, being careful not to note that he'd had his cock up the man's ass during the entire interview—he'd admit that to Kahn . . . maybe . . . but he wouldn't write it down—when the phone on his desk rang.

"There you are." It was Danny's voice. "I kept trying you on your cell phone and you've got it turned off."

"Sorry, yes I do. I didn't realize that." But of course he did. He hadn't wanted it to ring while he was working on seducing Garrison. "What gives? Where's everyone?"

"We're down here on the docks. There's been another one. You should be here."

"I'm on my way. Where, exactly?"

"Go to the end of Christopher Street, point your nose at the *Larnaka Star* where it's docked, and then you'll find us between some containers off to the right. You'll be able to pick us out because of the police cars and the bright lights."

"Right. What a surprise. Be there soon."

Clint just stood over the body of the beaten man when he got to the docks He didn't say anything until Danny nudged him.

"Yeah, I recognize him. From the interview yesterday that you conducted in the tombs. I guess it doesn't matter much to Brunelli—having his possible alibi bop out on him. He's not in the best condition today either." Clint was thinking on just how long it had been since he'd seen Greg Garrison alive. And he was remembering that Garrison seemed really alive, keyed up at having gotten his revenge on both Brunelli and Pendleton—not to mention a good fucking from Clint. Something inside Clint made him glad that Garrison had gotten his own before someone beat him to death and left him out here on the docks between two shipping containers half clothed.

Were these the same containers the stevedore had started fucking Clint between the other day? Yes, he thought they were— or ones that had replaced those. Was there any connection? Yes, possibly. Clint, the detective, wasn't about to overlook any possibility.

Danny was talking to Burton Kahn. "We need to know how long he's been out here, Lieutenant. And put a rush on the workup too. Brunelli was real pissed that this guy reneged on his alibi."

"You can't kill Brunelli again, Danny," Clint said, turning his head away from the corpse of Greg Garrison. "And you can't pin this on him either. You had Garrison in hand yourself yesterday when Brunelli was marched off to his death."

"It could have been one of his guys, though," Danny said stubbornly. "Maybe the bodyguard, Wilde, before we caught him."

"Wilde was caught so far down I-95 that he must have left as soon as we took Brunelli into custody. And Wilde's been in custody since last evening. Isn't that right, Lieutenant?"

"Yes, he has. And he's singing like a bird. We got the guy who knifed Brunelli too. It was an inside job. The bodyguard admits to setting it up, and he's saying that Hodgkins was in on an attempt to deep six Brunelli and take over his operation."

That's taken care of then, Clint thought. That was a main reason for me to turn in the summary of what Greg said. We needed to get the bodyguard and Hodgkins pinned down for their part in this. What he said, however, was, "Then the bodyguard is out too. I was with Garrison earlier today. I can vouch that he was alive at least until a bit after 5:00 p.m. So can others at The Dugout bar. He was working."

"And you went to see him?" Danny asked. Clint turned to see his partner looking intently at him. He was getting tired of Danny's attitude in all of this.

"Yes And don't hurry too fast on those lab results. Because when you get them, you'll find out that my DNA is in there too."

"Shit, Clint. You just can't keep your pants up, can you?"

"I don't see that that's any concern of yours, Danny." Clint shot back. "And I had my reasons, even though that don't seem to matter much anymore. But, keeping us on the important subject, my vote is that this was a another killing by the serial killer—that it had nothing to do with Brunelli. I say we get real justice for this man rather than just sweeping everything that comes along into Brunelli's grave. I say we get cracking on those interviews with the crew of the *Larnaka Star*." With that, he turned and walked away.

He walked and walked and walked. Unsure again whether his steps were taking him back to the squad room at the precinct, home, or to the gay bars to try to drown himself in mind-numbing sex.

When he reached the squad room, Clint went directly to his computer, which was still on, pulled up the file he had created earlier in the day, and pressed the delete button. Yet another judgment stolen, he thought. Without Greg being here to question, nothing that Clint had written could be taken as the truth.

"Note to self," he said aloud as he stood up from the desk in the deserted squad room, "never let yourself get this close to a case again."

"Another note to self," he muttered as he headed for the door. "Let's get wasted. Then let's get this serial killing pinned down."

Chapter Eight: Play time

What, again? Clint thought as he rolled over in the bed and encountered warm, hard flesh. His head was pounding. His ass was tingling too. Felt like a Mac truck had rammed itself up in there. He liked that feeling; seemed he spent half his life trying to open himself wide—with help, of course. He liked it better when the truck was still parked, though. And when it did a little rocking and forward and reversing in there. He rolled back toward the edge of the bed, ready to continue out onto the floor and stagger to the bathroom. A headache you wouldn't believe. But his eyes couldn't find the bathroom door where it should be. No, he didn't have to piss. Must have done that in the night. So there must be a bathroom somewhere. Smelt like lust, like heavy sex. Sweat. Cum. Needed the shower.

Shit. This wasn't even his own bedroom. Where had he gone after leaving the precinct last night? All he knew was that he'd gathered another grief yesterday to add to those he wanted to forget. It was another guilt-laden one. He'd pumped Garrison for information—using a goddam lie—and then pumped him and left him. Not long after that Garrison was dead. Was that in any part his fault? Was any part of that not his fault?

What bar had he wound up in? What sleazy hotel room? Shit, he hoped this wasn't the Christopher Hotel. But, no, what he'd seen of the Christopher recently had been refurbished. This one obviously hadn't been refurbished since the Hoover administration. How did they get those stains on the ceiling? Guy must have been a real gusher.

94

Well, it must have a bathroom. He sure hoped it did. Needed to get under a shower—and find some Tylenol. There had to be a bathroom here somewhere. First things first. Get out of the bed first.

He moved closer to the edge and began to swing his legs over the side. But a light brown arm—colored tattoos from here to there, a full sleeve of riotous color—reached over him and pulled him back into the center of the bed. No problem doing it at all either. Much bigger guy than Clint.

An Hispanic, Clint thought. Tattoos. Bulging muscles. Where was there a bar featuring Hispanic motorcycle gangs? Had the fuck been good? Important questions first. Did the size of the cock go with the size of the body? Hard. Young. Prime.

"Good morning, blondie. We fuck good. We fuck again." The voice heavily accented. Guttural. Commanding.

Without even getting a good look at him, Clint felt himself being pulled over on top of a prone, hard body, facing a pair of gigantic feet. Big hands at his waist settled him on the cock.

"Beautiful bod. You could be a star. Done porn? You fuck like you done porn."

Yep, big body, big cock. God, he's long, Young and hard bodied, Clint thought as he felt the cock slide up into him. No problem on the fit. How long ago since we did it? How many times? God, I wish I'd been there for it. I haven't gotten a good look at him. Who cares, with a cock like this?

Clint's knees were on either side of the big Hispanic's torso, folding his thighs down to his calves. He arched his torso back, digging his fists into the mattress on either side of bulging biceps.

Well, maybe just one good-morning fuck, he thought. The cock was in deep. He knew he'd enjoy it. He began counterthrusting, moving with the thrusting of man's cock. Groaning and grunting. Panting for it. Let's do this!

"Knew you wanted it. Couldn't get enough of it last night."

Condoms. Had they done it with condoms? Were they doing it now with condoms? Were they . . . ? "Oh fuck, yes. Oh, shit! Getitgetitgetit!"

The Hispanic hunk folded Clint back flat against his chest, one tattooed arm across his chest, a hand cupping his chin, holding the back of Clint's head into the hollow of his neck. The other hand went to encircling Clint's cock and stroking it to the rhythm of the churning of the cock inside Clint's channel.

The hand on Clint's cock. "Yesss! Fuck me. Fuck me hard!" Once that hand is on my cock, we gogogogo.

A hand pulling on Clint's right calf, pulling his leg out and unfolding it. Another hand doing the same with the other leg. How many hands?

Clint's eyes flew open. His eyes could hardly see the second man, holding his legs up and out with fists on his ankles. Hovering over Clint and the man under him. Moving his knees up on the bed on either side of the Hispanic's closed legs and between Clint's spread-eagled ones.

Another Hispanic. Chest a riot of colored tattoos. Black hair down to his shoulders. A bodybuilder's torso. Young. hard bodied. Prime.

"Oh, shit, no." Two of them. There are two of them! And the second one isn't going to wait for a solo turn. But, god he's got a beautiful body. It was coming back to Clint now. Big Mike's bar. The challenge. A double. Begging to be punished with a double.

He felt the bulb of the second guy at his entrance, above the already-sunk cock of the guy under him.

"Yes. Fuck me!" Clint cried out. "Get it in there! Both of you. Do it. Now! Shiiit Yessss."

The ultimate barrier against remembering what you don't want to remember.

* * * *

Clint thought about nothing at all—gloriously about nothing at all—as he double-timed it to his apartment, showered, grabbed coffee and a bagel while he dressed—Why does raw, brutal sex with two young studs make you so hungry? he mused—and then broke the speed limits, which is hard to do in Manhattan, getting to the precinct only slightly late—or as the other detectives would happily inform him, earlier than usual.

As he was climbing the stairs he permitted himself to ask the question. Did he regret it? That the answer, "not in the slightest," came so easily told him how much of a man slut he'd become. But just like a Mac truck ramming him up in there. Just like he liked it. And he hadn't thought about the death of Garrison—and so many others—while he was being driven.

He didn't go out to track down and interview the crew members of the *Larnaka Star* with the others. He grabbed at the duty to travel to Trenton, Maryland, after he arrived at work to hear the guys in the squad joking about how they'd tell Greg Garrison's parents how their son gotten beaten to death by fucking with the New York mobs. Clint believed that Garrison should have been brought to justice for what he did, but not the sort of stolen justice that he came to. And he certainly didn't think the parents deserved to be consoled with sneers.

To balance this, Clint volunteered to take the long drive to Trenton and, in giving the news, he didn't go beyond saying that he had known Greg and known him to be a man of loyalty to those he loved. He could do this with a clear conscious, because he knew that it had been loyalty to Greg's military friend from Afghanistan duty that had led Greg into everything else—and that he had persisted, regardless of the personal sacrifice, in bringing a sense of justice to that friend.

It had been an all-day trip. When Clint got back to the squad room, either the other detectives were still out running down *Larnaka Star* crew members or they were done for the day and had gone home. He sat for a while, still wondering if he'd done the right thing by deep-sixing his summary of the statement Garrison hadn't realized he was giving to the police. Who was he to be playing God on this? He knew that a good cop—or at least one who played strictly by the book—would write it up, give it to Lieutenant Kahn, and let whatever happened happen. But his squad didn't always play by the book. The very existence of his squad was something other than playing by the book.

But who was he kidding? After having visited with Greg's parents, Clint knew they didn't deserve any of the fallout that would happen if the police believed Garrison's unwitting testimony and confession and acted accordingly.

It had been a rotten day. It had been a rotten week. Clint needed to lose himself in a total fuck. What he had gotten this morning hadn't been enough; it hadn't been rough enough, even with the two of them. They hadn't punished him enough in the taking; they'd fucked for the pleasure of it—for the pleasure of all of them. They'd wanted Clint to enjoy it too—and he had. Clint felt the need to be punished, to be taken by someone thinking only of himself. Usually at these times, Danny would recognize the dark place Clint was in and would take care of him. Danny knew how to do him totally without leaving any bruises showing. But he and Danny weren't getting along very well just now—and Danny wasn't here.

Clint rose from his desk, left the precinct, and went to a subway station that would take him down to the docks area, to Christopher Street. He told himself that the other detectives might still be down there and that he'd join them, take report on what they'd found so far, and then join them. But his body knew better why he was going down there.

When he walked into The Dugout bar, he could see that the bartenders were moping around—just going through the motions—all affected in one way or the other by Greg Garrison's murder. Clint had told his parents that Greg was well liked by his coworkers. From the way they were behaving tonight—the night after his body had been found—Clint felt that he had been right, even though he would have said that to Garrison's parents regardless.

In contrast, the clientele was even more boisterous than usual. The Russian sailor and his friends were there, at a table in shadows at the back of the room. They were all keyed up. He could see the flashing in their eyes. They were louder than usual, and there were more empty beer mugs on their table than usual. They obviously were het up about something.

Clint wasn't in the mood for preliminaries. After getting a beer at the bar, during which he sensed all eyes from that table and from several other areas of the room as well, on him, he walked directly to the Russian's table, set his beer down, leaned down, lifted the Russian's chin so that he faced up, and took the Russian's mouth in his in a deep kiss. One of the Russian's arms went immediately around his waist and pulled Clint close in beside him. He cupped Clint's package with his other hand.

Coming out of the kiss, Clint said, in a husky voice in which arousal was obvious, "We always seem to be interrupted. I don't want you to think that it was my idea to stop you the other two times."

"So, you want Sergey's cock, do you?" the Russian asked in a beery voice.

"Yes, if you're Sergey, I want Sergey's cock. Want to go somewhere?"

"Yes. Soon. But I'm with my friends now and with my crewmates around me like this, I don't think anyone is going to disturb us. I want a taste now; then more later. Like I did last time, but with a later this time. You want to wait?"

"No," Clint said. "I want it now. Here. With everyone watching how good you do me." And he did want that. Part of the thrill was that, as he walked across the room, all attention had focused on him. He was a magnate for other men. When he was in heat, all men around him were in heat. He wanted them all to watch him get fucked, for everyone in the room, including him, to feel like they were fucking him at the same time. A double wasn't enough. He wanted it all.

Sergey had already been pulling Clint into his lap, facing the table. "Good, because I give it to whether you say yes or no."

The Russian's friends, including the Baltic hulk, who sat directly across from them, leaned into the table, eyes big and attentive, hands under the table on crotches, as the Russian pulled Clint's T-shirt over his head and palmed his pecs. Clint lifted his arms and locked a fist on a wrist behind the Russian's neck. Their lips and tongues met in a deep, wet, full-tongues kiss.

The Russian was moving his groin underneath Clint, letting him feel the rising strength of his cock. Clint had already been skewered on the cock once before, so he wasn't surprised at the size of it. Still, he gasped and groaned.

When they came up for air from the kiss, Clint muttered, "Don't make me wait. It's been a rough day."

"And you want I should take the roughness away?"

"No. I want it to be a rough fuck too."

99

"A taste now. Later I fuck you as rough as you can take. Maybe more."

The Russian growled to the man next to him, "Pants, Vlad," and the man fumbled at Clint's belt buckle and zipper and pulled his jeans and briefs down and off his legs. The Russian had unzipped himself too, and his hardening cock was inside Clint's butt cleavage, the upper side of the staff rubbing across Clint's entrance. The Russian pushed Clint's torso down on the table top with one hand on the back of his neck, while his legs widened and spread Clint's legs, and the Russian positioned his cock with the other hand.

"No, wait," Clint gasped. "A condom. Protection."

"I thought you wanted it now," The Russian said with a guttural laugh. "OK, OK. Vlad, anyone. Rubber. Now."

Five packets skidded across the table top between empty beer mugs from several directions.

"Want to see it in his face, Sergey," The Baltic hulk muttered, and the Russian wrapped one arm around Clint's neck and pulled his body up while the other hand positioned the cock head.

Then Clint was panting and groaning and whispering, "Oh fuck, oh fuck, oh fuck yes," as his channel was slowly lowered on the hard, thick staff. The grimace in Clint's face lit up the faces of the men leaning into the table. They licked their lips in arousal and moved their hands in their laps.

Clint sucked in his breath, feeling the loss, as the cock drew out of him. Then he cried out and gasped as it thrust hard and deep back up inside him.

"Rough like that?" the Russian asked.

"Rougher," Clint said with a groan. "Punish me."

"Want it deeper," the Russian muttered, and the men on either side of him reached down and each grabbed one of Clint's ankles and raised and spread his legs further. Clint grabbed the handles of the chair and began raising and lowering himself on the cock in rhythm with the Russian's grunting and upward thrusts, his hands now on Clint's waist, helping Clint to raise his channel up the cock and then thrusting down hard as Clint released the tension in his arms.

"You want it bad," the Russian muttered.

"Yes, I want it bad," Clint answered. He was screaming to himself in his mind: Harder, deeper, punish me, make me forget.

Vlad leaned over and took Clint's cock in his mouth and sucked him off, bringing him to ejaculation not long before the Russian gave an "Ufff," held Clint down into his groin motionless for a short minute, raised and lowered him slowly twice, and then jerked his pelvis three times.

They held there for a few minutes after the Russian had shot off.

"Is good?"

"Yes, is very good," Clint answered with a sigh.

"Is better without rubber," the Russian said. "You let me do it in hallway without rubber."

"We don't know each other that well. And I didn't have much choice in the hallway."

"We know each other better in a few minutes." Then the Russian lifted Clint off of him and turned him over to Vlad, who showed every desire of continuing with Clint himself, with Clint not showing quite the same interest in him.

"Hey, I got good cock too. I can show you good time too."

Clint didn't respond other than to brush Vlad's searching hands away. His eyes were following the Russian as he stood and went around the table. Clint believed the Russian could give him more of what he thought he needed.

The others at the table were still as statues, still leaning into the watching in their minds' eyes the fucking that had gone on at the table in the shadows of the bar room. The rest of the room was more quiet than usual too. Most—the ones who hadn't just arrived—had realized what was happening and some had tried to look on without those at the table seeing that they were interested.

The Russian reached the Baltic hulk and leaned down and whispered something to him. He straightened up then and said, "I go take piss now. Pietr here will see you not bothered."

As soon as Sergey was through the door to the corridor to the johns, the Baltic hulk, who Clint now knew was named Pietr, rose and came around the table.

"Put pants and shirt back on now. We go."

101

"Where?" Clint asked.

"We go to where Sergey fuck you good. Then maybe I fuck you good too. Maybe Sergey and me fuck you together."

Clint shivered. He didn't know if Pietr was saying this to frighten him, but it had the opposite effect. It's exactly what he wanted tonight. The same the Hispanics had given him, but with cruelty. Clint was sure that the Russian and his friend would be cruel. Brunelli had been cruel. That's way Clint had gone with him repeatedly.

The others started to rise from the table. "You stay," Pietr commanded. "Sergey say you stay."

Vlad reluctantly let Clint rise from his lap and then looked longingly at him as Pietr and Clint walked out of the bar.

"Where are we going?" Clint asked after they'd started walking. They were going in the direction of the docks.

"Sergey not tell me to take you—we go to the ship. I want you to see something. Sergey say he fuck you till you can fuck no more. Sergey crazy. I want to show you what Sergey wants."

"I don't know," Clint said, his steps faltering.

"You want to die? If not come see what Sergey does to men he fucks. Then we call police. I have enough of Sergey's ways. You happy I save you, then maybe you fuck with me. I fuck better than Sergey does."

He had a steel grip on Clint's wrist and Clint followed him, knowing where they were going.

No hands were on deck at the *Larnaka Star* as they walked up the gangway. Pietr led Clint down into the bowels of the vessel—down ladders, through narrow corridors, down other ladders. When Pietr pushed Clint into a small cabin down a long, dark corridor, Clint had no question that this was the killing room the detectives had found when they'd searched the ship.

There was a cot with cuffs at the four corners, blood stains on the floor, and a table with various instruments of sexual torture on it.

He had been with the Russian three times now. Three brushes with death. It had been a close thing each time.

He turned to say something to Pietr, but whatever he was going to say was knocked out of him. A fist slammed into his face and then one into his solar plexus, doubling him over. Then

102

another upper cut to his face and he went down hard on the floor. He felt the kick in the ribs . . . and then nothing.

* * * *

Clint came around and immediately realized that he was on his belly on the cot with his wrists and ankles cuffed at the four corners. He idiotically thought that the cuffs were so tight and rough that they'd bruise. Just like this serial killer's other victims. He was in pain everywhere along his body. The beating must have continued, Clint thought. What might be broken? Who the hell cares what's broken? This maniac is going to kill me.

There was only one area of his body that wasn't in the pain of a beating. It was his channel. It was filled with something more than even the Russian had. There was pain here too, but it was a glorious pain. Clint was getting a royal fucking. Pietr was straddling his hips and fucking him hard and deep, with long, deep thrusts of a thick cock. He had his hands around Clint's neck and was choking him.

Clint couldn't help himself—this was both his tragedy and his fetish. He was coming—prodigiously—and he knew that if he lived long enough, he'd come again and again. This was fucking. This was what sent him to heaven.

He realized that Pietr wasn't wearing a condom. And he knew he was beyond panic when he caught him thinking about the Russian, Sergey, saying it was better without a condom—and, from what he was getting from Pietr—Clint agreed with the Russian.

Pietr pulled his cock out of him, came at his entrance, and then slammed the staff home and resumed fucking.

How is he going to clean that up? Get rid of his DNA? Clint nonsensically wondered. The detective in him had his eyes scanning the room. There was a metal trough and a metal hose on a spigot over in the corner of the room. But could he get it all clean. Maybe he wore condoms with the others. Maybe I'm the last. Maybe he plans to move on now.

God he can fuck. God he can fuck.

This was what, in fact, would send him to heaven, he realized, as Pietr started working a plastic bag over his head.

He was gasping for air, the bag firmly covering his face. Then when he was about ready to give up, having come a second time—and so wanted to wait until he could come again—the bag was being jerked off his head, Pietr was screaming in some foreign language, others were screaming in English, and the weight of Pietr was being pulled off of him.

* * * *

"How did you find me? Were you following me?"

Clint had been unbound but still was on the cot, on his side, his legs across Danny's lap, as Danny held him and rocked him.

"No, jackass. We were following this guy—and the Russian too. From the interviews, we were honing in on one or the other. Quite a performance you put on in that bar."

"Then what took you so long to find me. I was choking here." He'd meant it to take the heaviness off the air, to keep from crying himself. But Danny took him seriously.

"Damn freighter's a warren of hallways and ladders. Even though we'd been here before, this cabin was hard to find."

"You weren't there. You weren't there when I returned from Trenton, Danny. I needed it, Danny. I needed it bad. And you weren't there."

"I've told you this is going to get you killed, Clint. You're a damn fine cop and an even better lay. But you keep looking for it like this and it's going to get you killed."

"I . . . I . . . can't help it, Danny."

"I know, I know. I'll just have to put bells on those balls from now on so that I know where you are—and who you're getting done by."

"But we caught him, didn't we, Danny? And it wasn't Brunelli, was it?"

"Yes we caught him. Thanks to you, this case will be iron clad. And no, it wasn't Brunelli. But I don't regret that he was put down."

"Neither do I, Danny. But it was a stolen judgment. It just isn't as sweet if it's stolen."

But enough of that, Clint thought. There was nothing he could do about anyone's justice now. He needed to think more pleasant thoughts. If the Russian wasn't the serial killer, Clint wondered if he was still waiting for him back at The Dugout.

About the Author

Habu is one of the pen names of a former supersonic spy jet pilot, intelligence agent, male model, movie actor, and diplomat. A wild youth in South East Asia was spent enjoying whatever sexual opportunities came his way, and much of his gay male writing is about recalling incidents from those days and inventing ones he'd perhaps have liked to experience. He now leads a very quiet and ordinary happily married family life.

An American, he is a published mainstream novelist and short story writer under another name and in another dimension of his life. He has written or cowritten (with Sabb) over 500 published short stories and nearly 100 published erotica e-books, primarily of gay fiction but also memoir, straight fiction and ménage fiction. His hand and creative writing can be seen in stories and books by habu, sr71plt, Dirk Hessian, Shabbu, and Stephen Kessel—among unrevealed others that might surprise readers. The fictionalized GM memoir *Flying High, Diving Deep* is loosely based on his life experiences. He can be found at the adults only gay male site www.BarbarianSpy.com, which he shares with Sabb and Dirk Hessian.

Our authors always like to receive feedback, and appreciate it when readers post reviews at www.goodreads.com, Amazon, and other sites.

BarbarianSpy
FOR LITERARY HEAT

Not all books listed below may currently be on release.
* indicates the book is available in paperback and e-book.

BOOKS BY DIRK HESSIAN

Xtreme Erotica
The King's Men
Shores of Tripoli
Prophecy of Noto
Pretender's Fate

General Erotica/Romance
Fire Down the Valley*
Constantinople*
The Beautiful Way*
Blue and Gray
Colonel's Treasure
Beginning of Time
Labyrinth

BOOKS BY HABU

Gay Erotica
Memoir Faction
Flying High, Diving Deep*
Xtreme Erotica
Apyko: The Greek Pimp
Visits of the Schlange
Second Coming: Emile La Cour Unleashed
Vortex: Sacrificed by Curiosity*
Dark Angel Sounding (*in e-book & included in Sounding:Ultimate Control Paperback*)*
Sounding: Ultimate Control (*Print Only*)*
Sounding Five (*in e-book & included in Sounding:Ultimate Control paperback*)*
General Erotica
Romance

Snowy, Snowy Nights (Christmas Romance)
Four Coins
Lower Than the Heart
Brambleton
Gotta Keep Trying
Finding Amnad
Platres Conclave
Other Novels/Novellas
Cruising Gigolo
Prepared in Cape Verdi
Gilded Cage
House on Park
Anything for Ambition
Dance of the Ravishers
Hard Knocks U*
My Neighbor's Spa*
Man's Man: Tales of a High Priced Gay Hooker*
Trip Money
Clint Folsom Mysteries Compendium Volume 1*
Death to Blonds - Stolen Judgment (Clint Folsom Mystery)*
Clint Folsom Mysteries Compendium Volume 2*
The Indian Doctor
Sailorboy
Home to Fire Island
Choke Hold
Gay Erotica Anthologies
Spy Tales 001*
Spy Tales 002*
Doubled*
Doubled Again*
Tails in the Tropics*
Tails in the Med*
Tails in the West*
Rough Riders*
Grab Bag 1*
Grab Bag 2*
Grab Bag 3*

Grab Bag 4*
Grab Bag 5*
Beyond the Beaded Curtain*
Habu's Christmas Balls
The Sporting Life*
Fetish Galore!*
Literary Gay Erotica
Cairo Surrender*
The Handyman*
Homeward Bound
Journey to Mirage*
Menage Erotica
Cruising Gigolo
13 Ways for Halloween
Luther*
The Indian Prince
Literary GLBT Fiction
Summer of Denial
BOOKS BY SHABBU
Finding Jason
Dirty Pool
Operation Black Jade
Cigars!*
Angel in the Barn
Gayly Complicated*
Despoiling David
The Tree of Idleness*
I Met a Man
The Interview
Rough Road to Happiness
BOOKS BY SABB
Hiring in Hollywood
The Legend of Holleystone Grange
Surprise Encounters
She is He
Wrong Man
Loyal to his King
Barbarian Tales - Book One - Traveler's Tales*

Barbarian Tales - Book Two - Journeys Begin*
Barbarian Tales - Book Three - The Inheritance*
Barbarian Tales - Book Four - Road to Persepolis*

www.ingramcontent.com/pod-product-compliance
Lightning Source LLC
Chambersburg PA
CBHW021929170626
46807CB00007B/3037